He remembered e[...] time together five years ago. Each sigh, each gasp. The angle of her head as he touched her, the flutter of her hands curling into his shirt. The agonizingly sweet welcome of her body.

This, though. The sheer delicious reality of having her in his arms once more—of her heat and softness against his skin, of her mouth trembling beneath his—beat the echo of those memories all to hell.

He knew it wouldn't last. It couldn't. In a moment, one or both of them would find a semblance of good sense and pull away. But for now, she was here in his arms and she was kissing him…and the prowling restlessness inside him quieted.

Dear Reader,

I sincerely love every hero and heroine I've ever created—flaws, foibles and all—but some seem to leave a more indelible impression on my heart than others. After I finished writing *A Cold Creek Baby*, I must confess to a few little qualms of disloyalty toward all my other heroes when I realized that Cisco Del Norte just might be my favorite hero ever (until the next book, I'm sure!). I adored this dangerous, troubled, mysterious man from the very moment I came up with the idea for this latest series of Cold Creek books and couldn't wait to tell his and Easton's story. I think I've received more mail from readers asking when I would finally write their story than about any other characters I've created! Through the process of writing *A Cold Creek Baby*, I came to love them both even more and was so happy to help them find their happy ending together…and to show Cisco the way home for good this time.

All my best,

RaeAnne

A COLD CREEK BABY

RAEANNE THAYNE

SPECIAL EDITION

Published by Silhouette Books

America's Publisher of Contemporary Romance

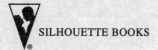

SILHOUETTE BOOKS

ISBN-13: 978-0-373-65553-3

Recycling programs
for this product may
not exist in your area.

A COLD CREEK BABY

Copyright © 2010 by RaeAnne Thayne

Visit Silhouette Books at www.eHarlequin.com

Printed in U.S.A.

Books by RaeAnne Thayne

RAEANNE THAYNE

finds inspiration in the beautiful northern Utah mountains, where she lives with her husband and three children. Her books have won numerous honors, including three RITA® Award nominations from Romance Writers of America and a Career Achievement Award from *RT Book Reviews* magazine. RaeAnne loves to hear from readers and can be reached through her Web site at www.raeannethayne.com.

Chapter One

Something yanked Easton Springhill out of a sound sleep.

She rolled over and squinted at her alarm clock, which glowed the dismal hour of 4:26 a.m. Her curtains were open, as usual, so she could wake to a view of the mountaintops still covered in snow. But from her bed she could only see a bright glitter of stars pinpricking the dark sky.

With a heavy sigh, she flopped back onto her pillow. She wouldn't be going back to sleep anytime soon, especially since her dratted alarm was set to go off anyway in little more than an hour.

What a pain. She really hated waking up before her alarm clock, especially when she had a feeling she'd been smack in the middle of some sort of lovely dream. She could only hang on to a few wispy tendrils of memory about what the dream might have been about, but she could guess that somehow *he* was involved.

She rolled over. Probably better, then, that she woke up. Whenever she dreamed of him, she spent the next day in a strange, suspended state—partly elated at having something of him again, even if only through her subconscious, but mostly depressed that she had to wake up and face the endless work of running an Idaho cattle ranch.

Alone, as usual.

The cotton pillowcase rustled as she shook her head a little, annoyed at herself.

She had a wonderful life here. She loved the ranch, she loved her friends, she had an honorary niece and nephew she adored.

So she didn't have the one thing she had wanted since she was just a silly girl. Was that any reason to fret and fuss and pine over the impossible?

She sat up, wondering what had awakened her. Jack and Suzy, her border collies, were barking outside, but that could mean anything from a loose cow to a hapless rodent foolish enough to enter their territory.

Whatever it was, she knew she would never go back to sleep now. Better to just take advantage of the unexpected hour to get some work done before she had to go out and take care of the chores. The Winder Ranch accounts were always waiting, unfortunately.

She slid out of bed and was just feeling around for her robe when she heard a sound that seemed to echo through the huge, empty ranch house.

She froze in the dark, ears straining. What the heck was that? It sounded like a cross between a shriek and a yowl. A moment later, something clattered downstairs, a jangly, ringing sound, as if a hard plastic bowl had somehow fallen out of one of the cupboards onto the kitchen floor.

Her heart pounded and her stomach curled and she wished she had brought one of the dogs inside. Since Chester, her ancient border collie who had been more pet than working dog, died over the winter, she had been alone in the house.

The ranch house sometimes creaked and groaned, as old houses were wont to do, but this was more than the normal settling noises.

She shoved on her slippers and grabbed the robe by her bed to cover the ancient John Deere T-shirt one of the guys had left years ago and grabbed her uncle's favorite old Benelli that Brant insisted she keep under the bed.

She lived alone on an isolated ranch where her nearest neighbor was almost a mile away. Only a supremely foolish woman would neglect to take basic defensive measures. She had been raised with three overprotective foster cousins and she was far from stupid.

About most things anyway.

Her heart pumped pure adrenaline as she fumbled for the shotgun shells in the drawer of her bedside table and loaded one each in the dual chambers.

As a precaution, she picked up her cell phone by the bed and slipped it into her pocket, not quite ready to call 9-1-1 yet until she checked out the situation to make sure she wasn't imagining things. She would hate having to explain to Trace Bowman why she had called the police to deal with a raccoon in her kitchen.

She pushed open her bedroom door, chiding herself again for her stubbornness in staying in her upstairs room after Jo died. It would have been more convenient all the way around if she had moved downstairs to one of the two bedrooms on the main floor, but she had been obstinate in clinging to her routine, staying in the same room she had moved into as a grieving, lost sixteen-year-old after her parents died.

She started down the stairs and had almost reached the squeaky stair that had caused the boys such headaches back in the day when she suddenly heard that yowly sound again. The hairs on the back of her neck rose and she gripped the Benelli more tightly.

That wasn't any raccoon she'd ever heard. Danged if that didn't sound like a mountain lion.

That would certainly explain the dogs barking. She thought of the tracks she had seen the afternoon before, but that had been clear on the edge of the north pasture, on the other side of the fence line.

Would a cat actually come into a house, even if she might have been foolish enough to leave a window open or something, which she was almost positive she hadn't done?

She had never heard of one of the big cats breaking into an occupied house. They were reclusive, wandering creatures who avoided human contact whenever possible.

A bit like Cisco.

See what dreaming about the man could get her? she chided herself. Even when she couldn't remember the content of her subconscious meanderings, she still spent the entire next day thinking about him, even at ridiculously inappropriate times like this one.

That couldn't be a mountain lion in her kitchen. She refused to believe it. Despite her usual precautions, she had probably just forgotten to close the kitchen window she'd opened to the May air and the breeze was moving the blinds, which were subsequently knocking down the hand lotion and soap she kept in the windowsill.

It was a good explanation and one she was sticking to. If it didn't quite explain the yowly sound, well, she wasn't going to fret about that, yet.

She reached the bottom of the steps and her pulse kicked up a notch. She could swear she hadn't left the kitchen light on when she went upstairs to bed. Part of her nightly ritual was to walk through the house to make sure it was closed up, the lights out, the doors locked.

She wouldn't have forgotten—and unless she was dealing with a mountain lion who had particularly dexterous paws, she doubted any animal turned the light on.

The tinkle of breaking glass sounded from the kitchen followed instantly by a muffled curse.

Not a mountain lion. Definitely an animal of the human variety.

Her hands tightened on the shotgun and she flattened herself against the hallway wall. Should she sneak into her office, bolt the door and call 9-1-1? Or stick around and hold the intruder at bay with the shotgun until the authorities arrived?

But what if there were more than one? No, her best bet was the office route. She could avoid the kitchen altogether that way and let Trace and his police officers handle things.

She took a step toward the office and then another. When she had covered half the distance toward the open doorway, she heard a tiny squeaky sound, almost like a giggle, and then a gruff voice in response.

A giggle? What on earth?

She knew two adorable babies with that same kind of laugh, but she hadn't been expecting either of them to be visiting her anytime soon, at least as far as she knew.

Joey Southerland, Quinn and Tess's ten-month-old, was sleeping soundly in his Seattle bedroom right now and little Abby Western was in Los Angeles with Mimi and Brant.

If not them, who was currently giggling in her kitchen?

She had to find out.

She heard another giggle, which made up her mind for her. She would call 9-1-1 after she figured out who was breaking into her house.

She inched forward, pumping the shell into the Benelli's barrel in that unmistakable che-che sound, then rounded the corner of the kitchen.

"If you make one move, I'll take you out," she snapped. "Don't think I won't."

After the dimness of the stairs and the hallway, it took a moment for her eyes to adjust to the light, before she could finally see who was standing in her kitchen.

The instant she recognized him, she knew without a doubt she would have preferred the mountain lion. When it came to dangerous beasts, any smart woman would far rather tangle with a ferocious carnivore on a rampage than the hard, dangerous man standing before her holding a...*baby*?

"Dammit, East. You scared the life out of me!"

Her cheeks suddenly felt hot and then ice-cold. This couldn't be real. Maybe she was still stuck in some weird dream about him. Why else would Cisco del Norte be standing in her kitchen holding a dark-headed pre-toddler wearing a pink velour sweatsuit with a bright yellow duck printed on the front?

No. The shotgun felt only too real to her, hard and cold and resolute, and he was definitely standing in her kitchen, though he looked bleary-eyed and tired, as if he hadn't shaved in days, and his clothes had certainly seen better days.

And he definitely had a baby in his arms.

She took another step into the kitchen, ejecting the shells from the chamber of the shotgun as she went.

"I just about shot your family jewels off, Cisco. What are you doing here? Why didn't you call me? And who's the...baby?"

The child in question giggled and Easton could see her skin was dusky like Cisco's and she had huge blue eyes with long, inky lashes that matched her curly hair and a couple of darling dimples in her cheeks.

She appeared to be around the same age as Joey and Abby, which would probably put her on the short side of a year—but then, Easton wasn't the greatest judge of those things. Show her even a photograph of a calf and she could guess how old it was within a few days either way, but human babies weren't as easy.

"It's a long story. I promise, you can put away Guff's Benelli."

She wasn't so sure about that and figured she would keep the shells close, just in case. "Maybe you'd better start at the beginning. What's going on, Cisco? You want to tell me why I haven't heard from you in months and suddenly you show up at the ranch out of the blue before 5:00 a.m., looking like you barely survived a tornado. And with a baby to boot."

He sighed and she saw new lines around his mouth, another thin, brittle layer of hardness covering the sweet charmer he'd been as a boy. He looked as tired as she'd ever seen another person.

"Sorry about that. We probably should have found a hotel somewhere on the way. But we flew into Salt Lake late last night from Bogotá and Isabella fell asleep in her carseat the minute I picked up the rental car. I just figured I would keep driving until she woke up, but she slept the whole way, even when I stopped for gas in Idaho Falls."

"Which explains exactly nothing, except that the baby's name is Isabella and you've just flown in from Colombia," she muttered. As he probably knew full well.

Cisco had always been very good at convoluting reasons, spinning stories and rationalizations until a person couldn't remember her own name, forget about any information she might be trying to squeeze out of him. His particular gift had come in handy when he was still in school, but for personal relationships, those who knew and loved him found it frustrating in the extreme.

"Sorry. What was the question again?"

She might have thought he was being a smartass—he had always been pretty darn good at that, too—if not for the utter exhaustion on his features, the gray cast to his normally dark tanned skin.

When he swayed a little and had to catch himself with his free hand on the edge of the kitchen table, Easton finally set the shotgun on the table and reached for the baby, so they both wouldn't go down if he toppled over.

She tried to ignore the sharp little gouge to her heart as the little girl giggled a greeting, at the soft, sweet weight of her.

"When was the last time you slept?"

He blinked at her, the lines around his mouth and eyes looking even more pronounced than they had a few moments earlier. "What day is it?"

She had a strong suspicion he wasn't joking. "Wednesday. And if I had to guess, I would say by your bleary eyes, it was probably Sunday or Monday when you last had the luxury of sleep."

"Not quite true. I slept a little on the plane."

The baby patted her little chubby hands on both sides of Easton's face and giggled again. She smiled in response, then shifted to glare at Cisco.

"What were you thinking? You could have been killed, driving when you're obviously exhausted. And with a baby in the car, too!"

"I was fine." He gave her a forced smile. "You know me. I can always manage to find my second wind somewhere."

No. She didn't know him. Not anymore. Once he and his foster brothers Brant Western and Quinn Southerland had been her best friends, sharing secrets, trading dreams. She had adored Cisco from the moment he arrived at Winder Ranch.

And then everything changed.

The baby grabbed a lock of Easton's hair and yanked. Everything inside her wanted to weep—and not at the physical pain. She couldn't shake the image of another beautiful dark-haired baby whom she had held for only a brief moment.

"Sorry to barge in on you like this, East. I should have called, but it was late when we got into Salt Lake."

Again, no real explanation about what he was doing there with a strange baby. He had become even better at evasive tactics, it that were possible.

"I didn't know where else to go," he continued. "Any chance you have room for us here at the ranch for a few days?"

She wanted to shut the door firmly against him— and especially against this little girl in her arms who dredged up old sorrows. But she straightened her spine. She was tougher than this. If she could run a cattle ranch by herself, surely she could handle a few days with Cisco del Norte and this mysterious child.

"You know you don't have to ask. It's only me in this big rambling house. There's plenty of room. And anyway, you know you own a part share of the ranch, just like Brant and Quinn. I can't kick you out."

"Even when you'd like to?"

She opted to ignore his wry tone as the baby beamed at her with a grin that showed off two tiny pearl teeth on her bottom gum.

"Is she yours?"

She was relieved to see a little color return to the gray cast of his tired features.

"No. Hell, no!" he exclaimed. "Don't you think I would have told you guys if I had a kid somewhere?"

She refused to think about the bitter irony of that. "You keep everything else from us. Why not this, too?"

Anger briefly broke through the exhaustion and flickered in his hot cocoa eyes. "She's not mine."

"Then where did she come from and what are you doing with her?"

His mouth pursed. "That is a really long and complicated story."

She said nothing, just waited for him to expound. That was a trick she had learned long ago from her Aunt Jo, who had always been eerily effective at letting her foster children dig their own graves with their words.

Cisco apparently wasn't immune to the technique. After a moment he released a heavy breath. "Her parents were friends of mine. Her father was killed right before she was born and her mother died last week. Belle's paternal aunt lives in Boise. Before she died, her mother begged me to bring her to the States to her family. Only problem is, the aunt's not available to take her for a couple of days."

She could find enough holes in his story for her to drive her shiny new Kubota through, but he was literally swaying on his feet. She had a feeling that meager information was all she would be able to squeeze out of him for now.

She really didn't want him here. Most days, she liked to think she was strong and capable, in full control of her little world here. Cisco only had to walk back through the door to dredge up all those feelings she worked so hard to fight back the rest of the time. She would have liked to tell him to find a hotel room somewhere, but she couldn't. Winder Ranch was as much his home as hers, even if he seemed to want to forget that.

"We can talk about this after you have a chance for some rest," she said. "Let me run up and put fresh sheets on your bed. Tess and Quinn have turned Brant's old room into a guest nursery for Little Joe when they visit and Abby uses it when she naps. Isabella should be able to stay in the crib there."

"You don't have to make the bed. I can take care of it. And right now I'm so tired, I would stretch out right here on the tile floor of the kitchen if I had half a chance."

"I know where everything is and you know you'll sleep better on clean sheets. Just relax for a few minutes while I take care of it, if you can stay awake that long."

"Thanks, East."

He gave her a guarded smile that didn't reach his eyes and she hated all over again the awkwardness between them, the tension that always seemed to hum between them like a tightly strung electric fence.

Nothing she could do about that now. She had lived with it for the last five years, since her uncle's death and the events surrounding it. She could live with it for a few more days in order to provide Cisco and the baby a place to crash.

She took a moment to take off her nightgown and robe and throw on a pair of Wrangler and a T-shirt, then brushed her teeth and pulled her hair into a quick braid before she headed for his old room.

Her Aunt Jo and Uncle Guff hadn't had the dozen children they had dreamed about to fill all the bedrooms of the old ranch house, so they had instead taken in troubled boys. Cisco hadn't been the first or the last, but the three of them—Quinn Southerland, Brant Western and Cisco—had been closer than real brothers. Their rooms had always been kept at the ready for their visits home.

She purposely didn't come into Cisco's room often.

She paid a young mother in town to come in once a month to keep the worst of the dust at bay throughout the house, which allowed her to leave his space largely untouched.

The room wasn't much different than it had been when he lived here with her aunt and uncle. Plaid curtains in dark greens and blues, a utilitarian chest of drawers, a desk and chair, a full-size bed with the log frame her father and Guff had made.

It was nothing luxurious, just good-quality furnishings in a comfortable space. How must it have appeared to him when he showed up, the orphaned child of migrant farmworkers who had moved him from town to town with them according to the harvest?

She had a vivid memory of the day he arrived. She had been just a kid. Nine, maybe. Her parents had been alive then and she had lived in the foreman's house just down the drive toward the canyon road. She had been sitting on the horse pasture fence rail watching Brant and Quinn work a new colt under Jo's supervision waiting for Guff. She remembered how her heart had leaped when Guff pulled up in the old pickup he kept scrupulously clean. He wasn't alone. A moment later, the passenger side opened and out stepped a dark-haired Latino boy in faded Levi's that were a couple inches too short and a thin T-shirt in worse shape than the rags her mother used to wash the windows.

They had known he was coming. Jo had told them all about the kid who had been found a week or two earlier living in a tent by himself in the mountains, where he'd hidden away from authorities after his father's death in a farm accident.

While she knew Brant and Quinn were a bit

apprehensive about a new arrival, Easton was excited to add another honorary brother to her growing collection.

She remembered sliding down from the fence rail and walking with Jo toward Uncle Guff's pickup truck, vaguely aware Brant and Quinn had followed.

Guff had come around the truck and placed a protective arm around Cisco's narrow shoulders. For a moment, Easton's heart had squeezed inside her chest at the expression in his eyes—lost and grief-stricken and frightened.

But then he suddenly gave a cocky grin that encompassed all of them. And she fell in love.

She still didn't know whether it was that quick glimpse of vulnerability in his eyes or his valiant attempts to hide it, but she vowed that night to herself that she would love Cisco del Norte forever.

Easton snapped one corner of a clean fitted sheet over the mattress. What kind of idiotic female holds to a vow she made when she was nine flipping years old? Twenty years later, she still couldn't get over the man.

She had been telling herself for years that this tangled morass of emotions wasn't love. She had tried to talk herself out of it—or more accurately *into* letting herself love someone else. It was only a girlhood crush, something most sane women put away when they reached an age of reason, for crying out loud.

Yes, they had a history together. She drew a shaky breath and tucked in the bottom sheet, her mind drifting back five years to that surreal, painful time.

Plenty of people with difficult histories were able to move on. She was trying. She was even dating again, something she hadn't been able to bring herself to do with any serious intent since the summer night after her Uncle Guff died, when everything changed.

For the past month, she had been dating the Pine Gulch police chief. On paper, Trace Bowman was everything she wanted. He was great-looking, he was funny, he adored his own family who had a ranch on the other side of town.

She was trying as hard as she could to let her fondness for him grow into something more. She wanted a husband, a family. Seeing Quinn and Tess together with their darling little boy and now Brant and Mimi and Abigail only intensified that ache to watch a child of her own grow and learn, to have someone else in this big rambling house to fill all the empty spaces.

She loved the ranch and found great joy in the hard work needed to make it a success. But she was ready for something more, something she knew she would never be able to find while she was hung up on Cisco del Norte.

She knew darn well she needed to move on. It was long past time. But every time she thought she was on her way, he showed up with that tired, cocky grin and those secrets in his dark eyes and she tumbled head over heels again.

Not this time. She pulled the thick Star of David quilt she, her mother and Jo had worked on the summer after Cisco came. She looked at the kaleidoscope of colors, the vivid blues and bright purples and greens. She could still see where her stitches had been crooked, amateurish compared to her mother's and Jo's.

She smoothed a hand over the stitches, remembering the time with two strong, wonderful women. After a moment, she tucked the edges in at the bottom.

She wanted to be tough like her mother and her Aunt Jo, to just forget him and move on. She almost thought she would have an easier time of it if he would only settle down somewhere instead of wandering from country to country in Latin America, doing heaven knows what.

If he ever stopped running, maybe she could relax a little, but she was never free from worrying about him. In all these years, he obviously hadn't managed to find whatever he'd been looking for or he would have given up that life long ago.

And when he was tired of wandering, he would come back to the ranch for a few days or a week, dredging up all these feelings again.

She wished she could just tell him to stay away until she got her head on straight. But how could she? Winder Ranch was his home, the first and only really secure haven he had ever known.

As much as her heart cried out for him to give her a little peace and leave her alone, she couldn't deprive him of that connection.

She couldn't turn him away, but she *could* control how deeply she allowed her heart to become entangled with him. This time things would be different.

She couldn't lose all the progress she had made to fall out of love with him. This time she wasn't going to let those feelings suck her back down again. She needed to move on with her life, to accept that, like that mountain lion she had seen prowling the edge of her property a few days earlier, Cisco del Norte would always be a wild, roving creature she couldn't contain.

Chapter Two

He shouldn't have come here.

Cisco sat at the kitchen table in the Winder Ranch kitchen, fighting his way through the strange and twisted mix of guilt and regret and pain tempered by the sweet peace that always seemed to engulf him whenever he drove through the gates.

He was so damned tired and the raw, gaping hole just under his left rib cage tugged and burned like a son of a bitch.

Like he'd told Easton, he wanted to just lie down right here in the middle of the kitchen floor and sleep for a week or two.

Belle banged her sippy cup on the tray of the high chair Easton had pulled from the utility room off the kitchen. "For Joey and Abs," she had informed him before she took off upstairs to do whatever she was doing with the bedrooms.

He shouldn't have come here, but he had spoken the truth to her earlier. He hadn't known what else to do, where else to go.

Like an idiot, he had been so sure he had everything figured out. He had originally planned to catch a direct flight to Boise, hand Belle over to her relatives, then head back without anybody knowing he was even in the country.

But when he finally was able to reach John Moore's sister just before his flight left Bogotá to let her know about Soqui's death and that he was on his way with her niece, she had been both shocked and distraught.

Seems that even as he called her cell number—information retrieved with no small degree of caution from the careful documentation Soqui had hidden away as insurance—Sharon Weaver was on her way to her father's funeral in Montana and wouldn't be back in Idaho for several days.

The news had thrown his plans into considerable disarray. He wasn't too proud to admit he'd been terrified. Yeah, he had somehow managed the wherewithal to take care of Belle in Bogotá for a couple of days after her mother's death without accidentally sending her to the hospital or himself to the nuthouse. But the idea of an indefinite stay with a nine-month-old baby in some hotel in Boise while he waited for Sharon to return sent him into a stone-cold panic.

Coming home to the ranch to spend those few days while he regained his strength seemed the logical choice.

Easton would know what to do.

That had been the mantra he clung to. She was always so in control of every complication. Even when

she was a little kid, she had been great at handling any
difficulty that came along, whether in school, with his
foster brothers or on the ranch.

He refused to admit that he returned to Winder
Ranch like the swallows at Capistrano because this
was home.

She was his home.

He touched the compass rose tattoo on his left forearm, the little squiggly E right over his radial artery that
connected directly to his heart, while Belle banged her
sippy cup on the edge of the table and giggled.

"You think this is funny, young lady?"

His voice was raspier than normal from exhaustion
and that stupid pain he couldn't control, but she didn't
seem to mind.

"Ba ba ba ba," she blabbered and he again thanked
heaven she was such an easygoing baby. He didn't know
the first thing about kids and wouldn't have been able to
endure even a few days on his own if not for Isabella's
sweet disposition.

Even though she quite obviously missed her mother,
she still was a sunny, good-natured little girl.

"You're glad not to be moving for a minute, aren't
you?"

She beamed at him, her tiny silver stud earrings
glinting in the early morning light.

Bringing her to the States was the right thing to do,
no matter how hard the journey to get her here had
been. With her last breath, Soqui had begged him, as
she lay dying from a gunshot wound to the stomach,
to take care of Belle, to bring her here to John's family
in Idaho.

He owed her this. She had faced danger with

astonishing bravery, had risked her life to finish her husband's work and to avenge his death against the drug lord who had killed him the year before.

Cisco had failed to protect her—big surprise there, since he had failed just about every woman unlucky enough to find herself in his life. But he would not fail in this. Soqui wanted Belle to be raised by her relatives in the United States and by damn, that is exactly what she would get.

Even if it meant he had to spend a few days at Winder Ranch fighting his demons.

Or fighting Easton, anyway.

Same thing.

As if on cue, she returned to the kitchen, bringing that elusive scent of mountain wildflowers that always clung to her skin. She had changed out of her night-clothes and into jeans and a T-shirt and pulled her hair back into a braid that hung down her back like a shiny wheat-colored rope.

She looked as sweet and innocent as the first pale pink columbines in a mountain meadow in springtime.

Ah, Easton. For a moment, the regret swamped everything else, even his worry about Belle's future. He missed her so damn much sometimes he couldn't breathe around it. Even on the rare occasions when he came home, he missed her—the real Easton, not this carefully polite woman he had turned her into with his stupidity and his out-of-control desire.

"I put fresh sheets on your bed. You're good to go."

"Thanks. I'm okay, though."

"Don't be stupid," she snapped. "Go ahead and sleep for a couple of hours. I can keep an eye on the baby while I work on ranch accounts, at least for a little while until Burt and the boys get here."

Burt McMasters was the longtime foreman of the ranch who had taken over the job after Easton's father and mother were killed in a car accident when she was sixteen.

Cisco had already enlisted in the Marines at the time of their accident and was stationed across the country. He had flown home for their double funeral and Easton's devastated grief had destroyed him. Completely wiped him out. The moment he walked into the ranch house, she had flown into his arms and sobbed as if she had only been keeping herself together until he showed up.

"I don't need two hours," he said now, pushing the grim memory aside. "Just one should charge me up for the rest of the day. If you don't mind keeping an eye on Belle, I would really appreciate it."

She gave him a critical look and he knew he looked like crap on a stick. He felt like it, too. His head throbbed and the quick sandwich he'd grabbed at an all-night drive-up somewhere in northern Utah sat like greasy tar in his stomach.

Easton opened her mouth to say something, but then shut it again abruptly. "Sure. Take an hour," she finally said. "Burt and I have some things to do later in the morning, but I'm free until then."

"I didn't bring Belle here to find a free babysitter."

"I'm sure that's true."

He could hear the unspoken question in her voice about why he *did* bring the baby there. He couldn't answer it.

His vision seemed to be growing hazy around the

edges and he knew if he didn't find a horizontal surface soon he was going to embarrass himself by falling over.

"Thanks, Easton. I owe you."

She didn't answer him, turning instead to the baby. He thought he caught something strange in her deep blue eyes, a shadow of an old pain, but she blinked it away.

"You're making a mess, aren't you, sweetheart?"

Belle giggled and clapped her hands. Easton smiled at the little girl, her features bright and lovely, and something hard twisted inside him, something he preferred to pretend didn't exist.

He turned away. "I only need an hour," he said again. "Thanks. And, uh, I'm sorry about this."

"Go to sleep, Cisco. I can handle things for now."

He nodded. She could handle anything. His Easton.

He wasn't sure how but he managed to make it up the stairs to his bedroom, although he was covered in sweat by the time he reached the top step.

It smelled like her in here, sweet and flowery. Perfect.

He ought to take a shower to wash off the travel stink before he climbed into those nice clean sheets, but he didn't have the energy. He would just lie here on top of the quilt, he decided.

Just an hour. That's all he needed.

An hour in a room that smelled like heaven and Easton—although, really, wasn't that the same thing?

"I'll be there when I can. I'm sorry, Burt. I didn't exactly expect this little complication today."

Easton swallowed her sigh at her ranch foreman's pithy response. Burt McMasters was a great ranch foreman—hardworking and dedicated, always willing to do whatever it took to get the job done. She adored him, colorful language and all, and without his firm guidance, she would have had to sell the ranch when Jo was first diagnosed with cancer.

But he did tend to be sulky and impatient when his plans went awry.

"Yeah, I know. It's a pain. I can't help it. Just start the immunizations and I'll be there when I can. Can you and Luis handle it without me for a while?"

"I s'pose." She could swear she almost heard the glower in his voice.

"You be careful up there," he went on in his gravelly voice that always sounded like he was choking on trail dust. "I don't like the idea of that boy being back in the house. I know Jo and Guff loved him just like the others, but in my book, that one has always been nothing but trouble."

She fought the impulse to jump to Cisco's defense. Yes, he had been fast-talking and imaginative and as a result he had managed to land himself—and the others—in plenty of mischief when he was a teenager.

Burt had never quite forgiven Cisco for a prank he'd pulled at their grazing allotment up in the high country when he had somehow convinced the prickly, proud ranchhand that he thought a black bear might be stalking their camp.

Burt had been deep in the woods early one morning answering the call of nature when Cisco had sneaked around behind him making appropriate bear grunting noises and Burt had come running back to camp in a panic, his pants half-down and biodegradable toilet paper flying out behind him.

For the most part, Easton would have to agree that Cisco was trouble. Except Burt was wrong about one thing: He was far from a boy.

"He would never hurt me," she blatantly lied, crossing her fingers behind her back. "You know that. He's family."

He harrumphed over the cell phone he abhorred almost as much as he did Cisco del Norte. "I still don't like it. Doesn't he know we have work to do around here? Maybe he's been gone from these parts so long he doesn't remember how busy this time of year can be on a cattle ranch."

She contained her sigh. "I'm sure he remembers, Burt. He lived here for a long time. But he needed a place to stay for a few days and this was his best option. He owns a good share of the ranch, don't forget."

"As if I could," he muttered. Easton would have smiled if not for the fretful baby in her arms.

"Look, I have to go. I appreciate you and the boys stepping up without me. I'll be there as soon as I can."

"Yeah, okay. Be careful," he warned again before ending the call.

Too late, she thought as she turned once more to the baby, who looked at her with huge blue eyes that swam with tears.

"I know, sweetheart. Let's get you a bottle and then we'll go see what's going on with that rascal Burt was just talking about."

She headed into the kitchen and found the can of powdered formula Cisco had left on the countertop.

Easton was grateful she'd had a little practice the last few months as honorary aunt to Joe and Abby or she would have been all thumbs with things like changing diapers and mixing formula.

She tested the temperature of the formula on her forearm, feeling a great sense of accomplishment at her own competence, then handed the bottle to the baby, who clutched it in her chubby hands and began sucking greedily, her darling cupid's bow of a mouth pursed around the nipple.

Something soft and tender tugged hard at Easton's insides. She settled the baby a little closer to her, trying not to look at the clock.

Three hours.

Cisco had promised he would be back downstairs in one. He lied, something he seemed to do with consummate skill.

Three hours and counting, actually, and Easton had work to do.

Not that there weren't compensations to this. Belle sucked her bottle a little more vigorously and snuggled her head closer to Easton's chest. Her eyes drifted shut, her eyelashes so long and curly that they looked almost fake.

She smelled of warm milk and baby shampoo, an intoxicating combination, and Easton inhaled like a wino fighting off the DTs.

Belle was by far the most sweet-natured baby Easton had any experience with. Until the last fifteen minutes when she started getting sleepy, she had been happy and smiling, content to play with a few of the other babies' toys Easton dragged into her office.

With those black curls, tawny skin and the shocking blue of her eyes, she was also remarkably lovely.

For three hours, Easton had struggled valiantly to tamp down the tangled emotions this little girl stirred. She had forced herself to focus on her care—changing her, playing with her, finding age-appropriate things in the house for Belle to explore.

She hadn't allowed herself a moment to think about the what-ifs that haunted her.

Now that the baby was asleep—or close enough to it—all those memories and regrets hovered just on the edge of her heart and it was becoming increasingly harder to keep them at bay.

She tightened her hold on the baby and headed in the direction of the makeshift nursery. Belle's long lashes fluttered when Easton began ascending the stairs, but then her eyes drifted closed again. They stayed that way when Easton carefully laid her on her back in the nursery crib. Easton pulled the bottle out carefully and watched Isabella's mouth continue to suck air for a moment before it went still.

She really was a beautiful baby, she thought as she pulled the baby quilt up and over her. What had happened to her mother? she wondered. Cisco said she was dead. How was he involved? He claimed the baby wasn't his, but with those long, inky eyelashes and the black hair with the tendency to curl, she could be.

After a moment spent gazing in adoration at the perfection of a nine-month-old baby, Easton forced herself to turn away. She checked the intercom Quinn had installed so he and Tess could hear their precious little boy in any room of the rambling house.

When she was sure it was on and transmitting any

sound coming from the room, she closed the door behind her and walked across the hall. She stood outside Cisco's door, her stupid stomach jumping at the prospect of seeing him again.

She hated this awkwardness, but didn't know how to change it. The events of the past were too deeply entrenched between both of them. After a moment of standing there like an idiot, she forced herself to knock sharply—only to be met by silence.

When he didn't answer, she knocked with a little more force. Still no answer.

She frowned. Cisco had never been a particularly sound sleeper. He always seemed to be on the edge of something fun and exciting. Jo used to shake her head and say he didn't sleep well because he was too afraid of missing something.

Even on roundup, when the rest of them would sink with exhaustion into their sleeping bags at the end of a long day, Cisco would be edgy and alert and would wake at the slightest distraction, even the wind rattling the tent.

She wrapped her fingers around the metal of the doorknob feeling foolish. Maybe he wasn't even in there. Maybe he had seized the chance to escape his obligations and climbed out the window. Wouldn't be the first time he had made use of the exit route along the porch roof and down the old maple that grew next to the house on the other side.

No. She couldn't believe it. He wouldn't just dump the baby on her and run. Cisco might be many things, but deliberately irresponsible wasn't one of them.

After a moment, she knocked harder. "Cisco? Everything okay in there?"

She thought she heard something inside and she strained her hearing. Weird. She could swear she heard a moan coming from inside.

Was he in the depths of some kind of nightmare? Even as disjointed as he tended to sleep, he hadn't ever been much to toss and turn. But what did she know? He wasn't the same person anymore, not with the hardness around his mouth, the secrets in his eyes.

The low moan sounded again from inside the room, unmistakable this time and Easton screwed her eyes shut, knowing in her heart she had no choice except to check on him. Either he was having a bad dream or he was in pain. Either way, she had to check out the situation, whether she wanted to or not.

She pushed the door open with caution and found the room dim, the curtains closed against the morning sunshine.

Her gaze flew to the bed and when her eyes adjusted she discovered he hadn't climbed out the window at least. He lay on the bed, a sheet covering his lower body, but he was bare from the waist up—bare except for a wide bandage wrapped around his stomach, a pristine white except for a kiwi-sized spot that was soaked through with blood.

His skin seemed even more pale and she could almost feel the heat radiating off him from here. On closer inspection, she could see his hair was damp with sweat and more drops of perspiration dotted the shadow above his upper lip.

She hurried to the bed and pushed back the hair flopping across his forehead. Even before she touched his skin, she could feel the fever pouring off him.

"Oh, Cisco. What kind of trouble are you in?" she

whispered. She didn't know whether to be scared or angry or worried sick.

"Can't. Oh, cara. Don't ask me," he muttered, his head tossing on the pillow. He said something quickly in Spanish she didn't catch.

She touched his shoulder and was seared by the heat of his skin. Had he driven here all the way from Salt Lake International, a good four hours away, in this condition?

"Cisco? Wake up. You're sick. We need to get you to a doctor."

He opened his eyes halfway, his lashes as ridiculously long and lush as Isabella's, then he uttered a long string of melodious words before he closed his eyes again. He had taught her enough gutter Spanish when they were kids that she caught the gist.

"Yeah, right back at you," she muttered. "Come on, wake up."

She looked at the bandage around his waist. Was it her imagination or had the red spot spread in just the few moments she had been in here trying to wake him?

She felt frozen with indecision. Should she continue to try rousing him or should she call the volunteer ambulance?

What if he had a gunshot wound? Weren't the medical authorities required to report those? What if he was tangled up in something illegal?

Drat him for coming here and complicating her world like this, forcing her to make decisions without any information to back them up. She had a deep, fervent wish that Quinn or Brant were here. They would know what to do.

"Cisco, come on," she pleaded.

Jake Dalton seemed her best bet instead of calling the volunteer paramedics. He ran the medical clinic in Pine Gulch and she knew he would be carefully discreet without breaking any laws. Only trouble was, she had no way to get Cisco into the clinic without a little cooperation on his part.

If she couldn't rouse him, she was going to have to call for an ambulance and if she had to guess, she figured they would probably opt to take him to the nearest hospital in Idaho Falls, about thirty miles away.

"Come on," she begged again, her hand on the hot skin of his biceps. "Please wake up, Cisco."

Those hot cocoa eyes drifted half open again. "Sweet, Easton," he murmured. "Smell so good. Like spring."

Some silly part of her wanted to stand here beside the bed and bask in his words like a wildflower opening to the morning sun.

Unfortunately, the rest of her still had to deal with their current predicament.

"Wake up, you idiot, unless you want me to call the paramedics."

Lines furrowed between his dark brows as if he couldn't quite make sense of her words. She opened her mouth to urge him a little further to this side of Sleepy Town, but before she could speak, one hard muscled hand snaked out and grabbed her arm.

"Hey!" she exclaimed, just before he tugged her across his chest, wrapped both arms around her and kissed her.

For perhaps a full ten seconds, she couldn't think beyond absolute shock. Dear heavens. How long had it been? He hadn't touched her in years, not once since that night after Guff's funeral. Not so much as a hug or a casual brush of his fingers on her arm or even a lousy handshake.

Finding herself in his arms again, his hard arms surrounding her, his hot, hungry mouth devouring hers, felt a little like jumping into a scorching hot springs after nearly dying of frostbite.

A woman couldn't be blamed for sighing against him, for kissing him back for just a moment. Right? Especially when it had been so very long.

She moved her mouth over his and her stomach muscles trembled with joy when his tongue dipped into her mouth, when one hand slid down her back to cup her behind and pull her closer.

Stop. The insidious little voice slithered into her brain. *He's only touching you because he's so out of his head he isn't thinking straight.*

Horrified at herself for losing all sense of self-respect, she wrenched her mouth away from his and scrambled out of his arms. "Cisco, wake up, damn you."

His brown eyes blinked all the way open. He stared at her for a long moment, his pupils huge. An instant later, he reached under his pillow and yanked something out and her heart stuttered at the sight of him aiming a deadly looking black handgun in fingers that shook with chills.

"S'wrong?" he asked in a dazed voice.

You came back. How's that for wrong? You came back and you kissed me and stirred everything back up again.

And then you pulled a gun on me, you son of a bitch.

She swallowed the words. "You want to put that away, cowboy?"

He shook his head a little as if to clear it and she saw him glance from her to the gun at the end of his quivering arm. Her heart fluttered with fear that he might accidentally fire on her. Wouldn't that be a fitting end? He might as well shoot her through the heart since he'd been stomping on it for years.

"East?"

"Put the gun away, Cisco," she spoke calmly, quietly, just as she would to a spooked horse. "Come on. It's just me. I'm not here to hurt you."

He didn't seem entirely convinced of that, but after a few more beats, he engaged the safety. She breathed a deep sigh of relief when he returned the weapon under his pillow.

"What's wrong?" he asked again, a little more clearly this time though he still slurred his words.

"You tell me. You're burning up and you seem to be bleeding. You need a doctor. I'm calling Jake Dalton."

He tried to sit up and because he wore no shirt she saw every muscle of his abdomen go taut—from pain or effort, she didn't know. That tattoo on his forearm rippled with the effort.

"Can't," he mumbled. "Too many questions."

In that moment, she hated him for doing this to her again. For coming home and dredging up all these feelings, for completely screwing up the sanity and reason she was trying so desperately to bring to her world.

For making her feel all these crazy, wonderful, terrible things again.

"I'm calling Jake," she repeated, her voice harsh as

she reached for her cell phone. "I don't have time to deal with a baby and a corpse at the same time."

"I'm not dying." He raked a hand through his hair. "S'just a little poke."

"A poke?"

"Knife. Bar fight. I've had worse," he said in what she assumed he meant as some sort of twisted comfort to her.

What kind of crazy life was he tangled in down there? For the last decade, her policy had basically been *don't ask, don't tell*. She hated him for that, too.

She narrowed her eyes. "Well, your little bar fight poke appears to be bleeding again and is most likely infected, hence your three-thousand-degree temperature. But that's just a guess. I'm calling Jake to be sure, so you'd better come up with a better cover story than a bar fight. I have a feeling he's not as gullible as I am."

He looked disgruntled, but didn't appear to have the energy to argue with her. "Where's Belle?"

She refused to be touched by his concern for the child. "Sleeping in the nursery next door. Guess I'll have to wake her to come with us. Look, do I need to call an ambulance or can you make it down the stairs and to my pickup?"

He released a heavy sigh. "I can walk," he muttered.

She had serious doubts about the wisdom of that, but knowing how stubborn he was, she was pretty sure he would manage it somehow.

His shirt hung on the slat-backed chair by the bed and she reached for it and handed it to him. He slid his arms in the sleeve only after great exertion. After she watched him struggle for a few more moments with the buttons, she sighed and stepped closer, doing her best to ignore the heat and pheromones radiating from him.

Just his fever, she assured herself. So what if he smelled so yummy she just wanted to stand here and inhale. She had more important things to worry about right now, like how in the heck she was going to move a hundred seventy pounds of delirious male down sixteen steps and outside without both of them falling down the stairs.

By the time he was dressed, Cisco wasn't the only one sweating. She felt like she had just roped a steer singlehandedly in the dark.

"Do you want to tell me again how you managed to drive all the way here from Salt Lake City?" she asked as he took an unsteady step toward the door.

"Wasn't that hard. Took I-15 to Idaho Falls and then turned right."

She glared at him, even as she leaned in closer to support most of his weight. "I'm glad you find this amusing. I don't. What if you had passed out? You could have driven off the road and killed both you and that darling little girl."

He made a face she assumed was supposed to look repentant. "Sorry, Easton. Shouldn't have come home. Not your problem."

He had made it her problem. As she contemplated the logistics of loading him to the rental car—better than her pickup, so she could put the carseat in the back, she had realized—she thought about how simple her life had seemed this morning when all she had to worry about were falling beef prices, rising feed costs, taking her cow-calf pairs up in the mountains, the creek near one of the haysheds that was about to overflow its banks and the capricious eastern Idaho weather.

Chapter Three

"A bar fight? That's really what you're going with here, Cisco?" Maggiee Dalton pulled the thermometer away and shook her head at the numbers there.

He could only imagine. He was on fire, burning up from the inside out. Another half hour of this and all that would be left of him on the exam room table at the Pine Gulch Medical Clinic would be a little pile of charred ashes.

He couldn't remember when he had ever felt so lousy.

Okay, maybe a few times came to mind if he jostled his recall. There had been that gunshot wound in Honduras when a stupid, spooked sixteen-year-old sentry had forgotten the password to the rebel camp he'd been infiltrating at the time and had mistaken Cisco for a hostile combatant. Okay he *had* been a hostile combatant, true enough, but the kid had no way of knowing that

when he fired on him with—unfortunately for Cisco—
better aim than his normal efforts.

And there was the time he had enjoyed a few delight-
ful hours of torture from a particularly zealous arms
dealer/terrorism financier in Panama after Cisco's cover
had been blown, before his support team could stage a
rescue.

This was right up there among his least enjoyable
moments. He was so damn tired, he just wanted to tell
Maggiee to go away so he could curl up on the floor
and sleep for a couple of weeks.

He couldn't seem to shake this woozy, out-of-body
feeling, the weird sense of disconnect.

"Yeah," he grunted, after a too-long pause while he
tried to collect his disjointed thoughts, for what they
were worth. "Little dump outside Barranquilla. Drunk
thought I was making eyes at his *señorita*."

"Were you?"

He might have been, if there indeed *had* been a bar
and a drunk with a knife instead of a brutal mid-level
drug dealer with more vicious machismo than brains.

"Don't remember," he lied. "I'm sure she couldn't
have been as pretty as you."

Maggiee rolled her eyes and yanked the blood pressure cuff tight enough that he winced.

Despite her current overzealous efforts to check
his vital stats, he liked Maggiee. Always had. She'd
been a couple years older than him, but he had known
her a little from school, back when she had been plain
Magdalena Cruz. Pine Gulch was a small town after
all, and her family's ranch had been on the same bus
route as theirs.

He had been sorry to hear what happened to her in

Afghanistan, especially when she had only been trying to provide medical care. Funny thing about that. He had been going through a rough patch of his own and had been on the brink of walking away from his complicated web of lies when Jo had told him Maggiee had been grievously injured in a terrorist explosion while she'd been deployed.

The news had shot new determination through him like pure-grade heroin gushing through his veins and he'd stuck it out a little longer.

Seemed a lifetime ago. She seemed to be getting around pretty well on a prosthetic leg, he was happy to see.

Or he would have been happy if he could manage to think through the pain and the slick nausea curling through his gut.

"You can try to sell that story of a bar fight if you want, but that doesn't mean I'm going to buy it," she said.

"You're a hard-hearted woman, Magdalena."

"True enough. Just ask Jake." She smiled a little. "And where does the baby come in?"

How did he answer that? Guilt twisted even more viciously than the damn knife wound. His fault. Soqui was dead because of him, that sweet little girl an orphan because he hadn't been able to protect her mama.

He should never have let Soqui in on the operation. After John's murder, she had begged him to let her bring down *El Cuchillo*. He should have just sent her to safety, maybe here in the States with John's family. Instead, he had used her fierce need to avenge her husband to help his own cover.

And now she was dead.

El Cuchillo's thugs might have fired the shot that killed her, but Cisco might as well have been the one holding the AK-47.

"Mother was a friend of mine," he finally muttered to Maggiee.

"Was?"

"She…died last week. But all the paperwork's in order, I swear. She gave me custody before she died."

He didn't want to close his eyes. He could still see that grimy warehouse, bodies everywhere—including *Cuchillo's*—Soqui bleeding out on the concrete.

She had known. He didn't know how, but somehow she had sensed they were walking into an ambush. Maybe she had known it would end like that from the moment she begged him to be part of the operation, months ago.

"I have papers," she had rasped out, her voice already thready and weak as her life ebbed away. Her hand was icy cold in his and each word seemed to choke her throat.

"Hidden under the…sink. Custody papers. Take my sweet Belle to Johnny's family. Where she'll be…safe. Swear to me, Francisco."

Her voice seemed to echo in his aching head, heavy on the reverb.

How could he refuse? He owed her this much at least. He had failed to protect Soqui, but he would do whatever it took to take care of her little girl.

"All legal, Maggiee," he said now. Technically, anyway.

Yeah, he had been forced to move both heaven and hell with a couple different embassies to speed up the process and had pissed off about a dozen agencies, but nobody could find any legal loopholes. He was Isabella's legal guardian until he signed custody over to her family. Whenever that happened, the sooner the better.

"She has an aunt. Boise. She's coming to take her in a few days."

Maggiee probed around the six-inch gash just below his rib cage. Though her movements were gentle, he was desperately afraid he was going to pass out.

Big, bad super spy. That was him.

"I'm sorry. I'm just trying to clean things up a little before Jake comes in to take a look."

"S'okay," he lied.

"Why didn't you have this looked at in Colombia?"

Because he was too busy getting Belle out of the country before *Cuchillo's* psycho baby brother discovered her existence—and before all the people he bribed or threatened changed their minds about letting him leave with her.

"Then I would have missed your tender, loving care, Mag."

She shook her head, even though she was smiling.

That was him. Always good for a laugh.

"What happens after Jake patches you up? You go back for more bar fights in some seedy cantina somewhere? Maybe next time with someone who has better aim?"

Damned if he knew. He was so tightly tangled in the web of lies he had spun that he didn't have the first idea how to break free.

El Cuchillo hadn't killed him, but Cisco was pretty sure it was only a matter of time before someone else would. He didn't have a death wish. Far from it. But after the last ten years of deep undercover work against narcoterrorism, pragmatism was unavoidable.

He figured he was lucky he'd made it this long.

Maggiee tilted her head to study him. Too damn smart, that Maggiee Cruz Dalton.

"Hear you've got a couple cute kids."

As a distraction ploy, it was pretty transparent but under the circumstances, it was the best he could manage.

"We do. One of each. A girl, Sofia, and a boy, Charlie. They keep us hopping."

"Sounds good." Would she mind if he checked out for a while? he wondered. It was all he could do to keep his eyes open.

"Maybe you ought to think about sticking around for a while while you recover from your bar fight. Easton is alone too much in that big old ranch house since Jo died."

He didn't need her laying that sort of guilt on him. He managed to pile on enough of his own, thanks.

"She's not alone all the time. Mimi and Brant spend time with her when they come back, now that Brant's stateside," he answered. "So does Quinn and his family."

He was the proverbial prodigal foster kid. The one Jo and Guff had always worried about the most. He regretted that, though before Jo died, he had finally told her the truth about his life and what he was doing. He knew a few hours' conversation couldn't make up for years of worry, but it was the best he could do.

"Family is everything," Maggiee answered. "I've

learned the last few years that we have to grab every moment with them."

He thought of his strange family. Jo and Guff had taken a group of lost, troubled kids without much hope. Juvenile delinquents, orphans, abuse victims. Yet somehow they had managed to form a family.

Easton had always been their heart. Even when she was a blond, pigtailed brat who followed the older boys around. Without conscious thought, he pressed a finger to the E on his compass rose tattoo.

"You're not going to pass out on me, are you?" Maggiee asked.

"You kidding?" he managed a grin, though it took just about all his remaining energy. "And miss a minute of a pretty nurse fussing over me? What kind of idiot do I look like?"

"Like an idiot who found himself on the wrong end of a sharp stick," a man's voice interjected. "And who might just find himself even worse off if he doesn't stop flirting with my wife."

He looked toward the sound, then winced at the pain in his head from the abrupt movement. Jake Dalton, Pine Gulch's only doctor, stood in the doorway, giving him a mock glower.

"Hey, Doc. Long time."

Jake stepped into the room and scrubbed his hands at the sink. "Yeah, I think the last time was when you toilet-papered my pickup truck once when I came home from college."

He supposed it was a good thing Jake was a dedicated doctor who wouldn't let Cisco's assorted past sins keep him from providing quality medical care.

But then, he didn't know the half of them.

* * *

"He belongs in a hospital, doesn't he?"

Jake's blue Dalton eyes narrowed and he pursed his lips. "Let's just say I'm not admitting him at this time," he answered carefully.

"That's not an answer."

"East, you know I can't say anything more because of privacy laws. It's the best I can do. I'm sorry."

She made a face. As much as she liked Jake Dalton personally, she hated all he represented. Doctors, hospitals, that distinctive smell of antiseptic and illness that lingered, no matter how one tried to wash it away.

Loss.

Seemed like every time she had any dealings with the medical community, she ended up losing someone, starting with her parents' accident when she was a silly, giddy sixteen-year-old who thought she had total control of her universe.

Her father had died instantly that stormy January night when their car had slid head-on into an oncoming semi.

Her mother had survived the accident—barely— and had been airlifted to the hospital in Idaho Falls. Easton's aunt and uncle had rushed her there to be at her mother's side, but Janet Springhill had died on the operating table.

Then had come Guff's heart attack. She had been the one to find him collapsed on the barn floor, clutching his chest. She had performed CPR while waiting for the paramedics to get there and had been able to get a pulse, but he had died on the way to the hospital in Idaho Falls. Easton, following behind the ambulance, had arrived in time for the grim news in the E.R.

Jo had been treated at the same hospital for the cancer that eventually claimed her life eighteen months ago. Whenever Easton had walked through the doors of that place to take her to chemotherapy or for an appointment with her oncologist, her stomach would churn in a conditioned reflex.

In another hospital room in another city hundreds of miles away, she had endured the most painful hours of her life. She couldn't even think about that time without her breath catching in her throat.

So much pain and loss.

She knew hospitals also brought forth life. She had been there when Mimi's sweet little Abby came into the world. And she imagined some hospital in South America had contributed to the birth of the little girl who was currently babbling on her lap.

"He insists he won't go to a hospital. I agreed to follow his recovery here as long as he's got someone to keep an eye on him."

She supposed that meant her. "What sort of care will he need at home?"

"He mostly needs someone who can make sure he takes things easy and doesn't overdo."

"That's a great plan in theory," she muttered. "I have a feeling it won't be so easy to implement."

"Do what you can. Rest is the best thing for him to fight the infection and heal. And I need to know immediately if his fever spikes again."

"Okay."

Jake gave her a careful look, his handsome features concerned. She had seen that expression before. One of the things she loved about Pine Gulch's only doctor was his concern not only for his patient, but also for those charged with their care at home.

"I could give the same advice to you," he said in that calm, reassuring voice of his. "Don't overdo, East. I'm sure we could find somebody in town willing to come out and help you with the little one there."

The suggestion made sense. Heaven knew, she had enough to do at the ranch without throwing in the complication of caring for a needy baby and a recalcitrant patient.

On the other hand, Cisco had come to *her* for help. Right now he needed her, when he had made a point of not needing anyone for the last decade or so. She wasn't about to surrender that to someone else.

"I'm sure I can manage for a few days. I've talked to Burt and he and the boys can pick up the slack for me for a while."

"Are you sure?"

"Stop worrying about me, Dr. Dalton. I'm not your patient." She smiled to let him know she still appreciated his concern and was warmed when he pulled her into a quick hug, baby and all.

During Jo's long illness, Jake had been a rock, always willing to come out to the ranch to oversee her care.

If not for him and the hospice nurse, Tess Claybourne—now Southerland who had married Easton's foster brother and distant cousin Quinn—Easton wasn't sure she would have found the strength to make it through those last difficult days of Jo's life.

"You take care of yourself, Easton. You have a bad habit of worrying about everyone else but yourself."

She snorted. "Yeah and I'm the only one in this room with that particular shortcoming, aren't I, Dr. Dalton?"

"Smarty. Just make sure he takes his medicine and promise you'll let me know if his condition changes or if you have any questions."

"I will."

"He should be out in a minute."

"Thanks, Jake."

He smiled in response, then left the waiting room to return to the treatment rooms. Life as a small-town doctor probably rarely offered him a quiet moment, especially with Jake's passion for his patients.

"He's a nice man, Belle. That's the kind of guy you should look for when you grow up. Someone kind and loving and dependable."

The baby beamed in response to her observation and squealed with approval before she turned back to sucking on a key from the plastic toy ring Easton had found in the diaper bag Cisco had provided.

Easton smiled at her, even as a cautious part of her warned her to steel her heart. She feared she was already dangerously close to falling hard for this little girl with the sunny disposition and the cheerful smile.

And wouldn't that be foolish? Belle would only be here for a few more days before her aunt came for her. Easton certainly didn't need more loss in her world.

She was still worrying about that when the outside doors to the clinic opened and a tough, rugged-looking man in the brown twill uniform shirt of the Pine Gulch Police Department walked through.

His green eyes lit up when he saw her.

"Easton! This is a surprise!" Trace Bowman exclaimed as he strode toward her.

He leaned in to kiss her cheek, his slight dark stubble a tiny rasp against her skin. He always smelled so good, like laundry soap and starch and some sexy but understated aftershave. It was one of the things she had noticed first when they started dating a month ago.

"What's going on? Are you sick? And who's this little sweetheart?"

Belle gazed at him in fascination, then giggled when he made a funny face at her.

"Um, it's a really long story." Now why did that sound familiar? Cisco wasn't home five hours before she was picking up bad habits from him. "I'm not sick. What about you? What are you doing here?"

He shifted his weight. "I just needed to interview Jake about one of his patients last week. He suspected abuse and asked me to look into it, so I was passing on the results of my investigation."

For just a moment as she looked into his warm green eyes, Easton wanted to smack Cisco for coming back just now. She and Trace had been on five dates and he clearly wanted more. She liked him very much, more than any other man she'd dated in…well, ever.

What wasn't to like? He was a good conversationalist, he cared about her opinions, he was reliable and safe and spent his days helping other people. Everyone in town liked Trace and his brother Taft, who served as the town's fire chief.

Easton had nursed secret hopes that maybe she could fall for him. She had been trying, had given him far more of a chance than anyone else she had dated.

Wasn't it just like Cisco to blow back into town just when she was working so hard to forget him with someone else?

She sighed. "Actually, I'm glad I ran into you. I'm

afraid I have to back out of our plans for Friday. I'm so sorry. I was really looking forward to it."

He looked gratifyingly disappointed. "No problem. We can always reschedule. There will be other movies and it's no big deal to cancel the dinner reservation in Jackson Hole. What's going on? Everything okay?"

Not even close. For one crazy moment she wanted to cry at the quiet concern in his voice and his expression. For all his rugged masculinity, he was a nice person who genuinely cared about his community.

She really wanted to fall in love with him—but the reason why she had been forced to try so hard at it suddenly walked through the waiting room doors.

Cisco looked slightly better than he had going in, although his complexion was still pale despite his light olive skin and his eyes looked tired.

Somehow he managed to look dangerous and disreputable, with his shaggy hair and his few-days-old stubble—especially when Easton compared him to Trace in his law enforcement uniform with his square jaw, sun-streaked brown hair and all-American good looks.

Belle gurgled and clapped her pudgy little hands when she saw him. Easton wanted to hold her close, to warn her to keep her little heart safe from men like him.

She realized she was standing a little closer than necessary to Trace and she eased back a step , but not before she thought she saw something flicker in Cisco's eyes for just a moment, then flit away.

He turned to Trace with a polite smile. "Hey, Bowman."

Trace didn't look any happier to see Cisco. A muscle

jumped in his jaw and his eyes clouded. "Del Norte." His voice was as cool as his eyes. "Last I heard, you were in some jail cell in Guatemala."

Guatemala? Jail cell? She hadn't heard about that one and she wondered, briefly, why Trace knew and she didn't.

"They let me out," Cisco answered with a small, slightly bitter smile. "Good behavior and all that."

A startling animosity crackled between the two men and even Belle must have sensed it. She fretted a little and Easton shifted her to her other hip.

Cisco turned to her. "I'm done here, East. You ready to head home?"

Why did he deliberately emphasize the last word there?

"I...yes. I just need to grab Belle's things."

"I'll wait for you in the car."

He turned rather abruptly and pushed through the double doors to the parking lot. Even though he seemed to walk at his normal pace, she thought his movements were more precise than normal.

Trace frowned at his receding figure, then turned back to Easton with one eyebrow raised. "You weren't kidding about the long story. Anything that involves del Norte must be as tangled as a rope ladder in a windstorm."

"I'm sorry." She didn't know exactly what she was apologizing for—breaking their date or the harsh reality that some corner of her heart would never be completely free to give to him or anyone else because she had loved Cisco del Norte for most of her life.

Unfortunately for her.

Because that was just the kind of guy he was, he

picked up Belle's car seat the moment Easton buckled her into it to carry her out to the car.

He opened the door for her and she picked up the diaper bag and Belle's blanket and walked outside. She wasn't quite sure where the morning had gone, but it was after lunchtime and the afternoon air was sweet with spring and smelled of lilacs and the early climbing roses that grew along the fence line around the medical clinic's parking lot.

"Be careful with him, East," Trace spoke before they reached their parking space, his eyes an uncharacteristically hard green glitter. "He's always been trouble."

Yeah, she'd heard that today. Since she didn't feel like arguing—and probably couldn't come up with any kind of valid evidence to the contrary, even if she wanted to—she opted to keep her mouth shut.

"Is he staying at the ranch?"

"Only for a few days. He's…healing from an injury and then he's going to be taking Isabella here to her family members in Boise. I'm sure he won't be here more than a week. He never is."

That muscle worked in his jaw again. "Why does he have to stay at Winder Ranch? Isn't there anywhere else he could go?"

"It's his home. Jo and Guff left him a share of the ranch, just as they did Quinn and Brant and me."

Easton inherited the majority share, fifty-one percent, since a portion of that had been passed to her from her parents. Quinn, Brant and Cisco split the remaining forty-nine percent, although since Jo's death, they had left all decisions to her and had refused to take any profit from the operation.

"Maybe you ought to try buying him out. I'm sure a guy like him can always use some ready cash."

She had thought of the same idea before but never acted on it, something that shamed her because she knew exactly why she hadn't made the suggestion. If she bought his share, he would have no reason to come back.

What did it say about her that she tried to convince herself she didn't want him to come back but she wouldn't take the one step that would be sure to keep him away? Even after everything that had come between them, she couldn't take that final leap to ensure he maintained the safe distance she thought she wanted.

"I really am sorry about breaking our date." She quickly changed the subject. "I'll make it up to you when things settle down a little, I swear."

She could see from the look in his eyes that he wanted to say more, but to her vast relief, he held his tongue. Instead, he pulled her into a quick one-armed hug since he was holding Belle's car seat in the other.

Before she quite realized his intention, he leaned down to kiss her.

He had kissed her before but never with this quite apparent stamp of possession. His mouth was hard, determined on hers and she held her breath, desperate to feel something more than this warm, comfortable stirring in her stomach.

Again, what did it say about how messed up she was that she just about imploded from Cisco's half-delirious kiss this morning but couldn't seem to sum up more than a mildly pleasant reaction when she was kissing the man she wanted so fiercely to care about?

She finally pulled away, uncomfortably aware that Cisco was inside the car watching them out of those brooding dark eyes.

"I better get this young lady buckled in," she said.

"Sure. Let me know when things settle a bit," he said with that easy smile of his. "I'll be looking forward to our date. Meantime, call me anytime. I mean it. I can be at Winder Ranch in a heartbeat."

What did he think was going to happen? Did he expect Cisco to bring in a gang of outlaws to camp out in Jo's vegetable garden?

"Thanks, Trace."

He watched while she fastened the car seat into the back of the car, then waved them off and headed back to the clinic.

When she had checked and rechecked the seatbelt and she knew she couldn't put off facing Cisco another moment, she slid into the driver's seat.

His features were veiled, his expression inscrutable as she started the car and pulled out of the parking lot. Only after they drove through town and headed up Cold Creek Canyon did he speak.

"So are you and Bowman a thing now?"

Her fingers clutched the steering wheel. "I don't know if I'd call it a *thing*, exactly. We've dated a few times, that's all. I like him."

"He sure looked like a dog marking his turf."

"A lovely picture," she muttered. "Regardless, you're imagining things."

"Am I?"

"I'm no one's turf."

She belonged to herself—all except for that stupid little piece of her heart that would always be Cisco's.

Chapter Four

This must be heaven.

He was riding his favorite gelding, a sure-footed roan named Russ, up a gorgeous trail into the Tetons. The mountains soared up ahead, sharp and angular and breathtakingly beautiful. The sky beamed on his shoulders and the air was delicious, the citrusy tang of pine mingling with the sweet scent of early wildflowers.

Of Easton.

She rode behind him on her sturdy little gray Lucky Star and when he turned around to watch her, she beamed at him, her waterfall of honey-blond hair rippling in the breeze.

She looked young and sweet and so damn happy. He hadn't seen her like that since, well, too long.

A perfect day. He wanted it to go on forever.

But nothing lasted. Suddenly the sun slid behind a

cloud and the trail turned dark and hazardous. Easton's horse slowed and the distance grew between them.

He had to keep going. Just a little farther and they could find shelter, out of what was now punishing rain.

But the trail criss-crossed a treacherous scree. His horse barely made it past the danger spot before part of the trail gave way in a shower of rocks and mud—and suddenly he could see Easton's horse step onto the thin trail through the rockfall.

"No. Stop. Go back," he yelled, waving his arms, but suddenly the wind seethed and churned around them and his voice was lost.

Easton smiled at him again, just before her horse slid down the mountainside.

He cried out in anguish…and his own voice must have awakened him.

He woke in an instant, already reaching for the 9 mm he kept under his pillow. In that instant between sleep and complete wakefulness, he scanned the room, muscles tensed and ready for any threat.

No. Just a dream. He was in his old bedroom at the ranch. There were the curtains Jo sewed for him and the light fixture with the wrought-iron brands around the base.

He put the safety back on the gun and slipped it under his pillow again while he waited for his heartbeat to slow, for the relief to course through him.

It was just a dream. Easton was safe. She hadn't followed him into a nightmare. This time anyway.

About the time his breathing started to slow and his pulse settle, he heard a tiny mewling sound. It took a moment for him to realize it was coming from the intercom.

Belle. That must have been the sound that awakened him.

He slid from the bed, ignoring the screech of pain, and made his way through the darkness to her bedroom next door.

Easton's bedroom was dark and he hoped it stayed that way. Belle was his responsibility. He had already pawned her off on Easton enough through the last two days. To his chagrin, he'd mostly been out of it since yesterday when he'd visited Jake Dalton's office, when he had teased Maggiee and seen Trace Bowman give Easton that deliberately possessive kiss.

After they returned to the ranch house, he had barely managed to make it upstairs to crash in his bedroom, where he was embarrassed to have slept round the clock. This damn fever and the heavy-duty antibiotics had completely wiped him out. Today he'd slept most of the day as well, waking up only a few times to eat and for a couple hours in the evening to play with Belle and help at bedtime as much as he was able—which wasn't much.

The moment she was asleep, he crashed again, though he had to wonder if all his dreams were as tortured as that one.

Yeah, he got it. He was bad news for Easton and she was much safer when he kept his distance from her. He really didn't need some shrink mumbo-jumbo dream analysis to figure it all out.

He moved closer to the crib. From the glow of the nightlight and the moonbeams streaming in through soft green-and-yellow curtains, he could see Belle wasn't completely awake, mostly whimpering in her sleep.

Whether she was giving a full-fledged tantrum or a tiny peep, it still made him break out in a cold sweat. He had no idea what he was doing with her. The week since Soqui's death had been one of the hardest of his life and he still couldn't believe he'd somehow managed to stumble through it.

She had rolled to her side and he pressed a hand on her back and hummed snatches of a half-remembered song. He didn't know where the lullaby came from. His mother, he supposed, though he could scarcely remember her since she drowned when he was three.

He didn't remember much of that either, but he'd heard the story often enough from his father that the events seemed vivid in his mind.

His parents had been migrant farmworkers traveling the country with whatever crop was ready for harvest. Lettuce, strawberries, cranberries, apples. Wherever their green cards would take them.

It hadn't been an easy existence. The pay was subsistence wages and their housing had usually been lousy, dilapidated shacks, tumbledown fifth wheels.

He had been born somewhere in Texas and his parents had always taken him along with them while they sought work. According to Papi, usually Cisco had been a good boy and stayed close to his mother out in the field, but one day he had wandered away while they were working the Gilroy, California, garlic harvest.

When she noticed him gone, Mariana had rushed to find him—and spied him just as he slipped over the edge of a wide concrete irrigation canal, running heavy and high from a recent storm.

She had rushed in after him, even though she didn't know how to swim. Somehow she had managed to grab him in the water and boost him to a flow control grate, where by some miracle he was able to cling until help arrived, but Mariana had been swept away.

He scrubbed at his eyes. He didn't remember much about that day. If he tried hard, he could dredge up a memory of the breathtaking cold and his fear and then the confusion when his mother never came back.

His father had never blamed him for causing his mother's death—and, he would later learn, the death of his unborn sister. Not in words anyway. When Cisco grew old enough to understand, he blamed himself, though. What kid wouldn't?

When he got a little older, he used to imagine he had been the one to rescue his mother, at immense danger to himself. Somehow he had swept in and plucked her from the waters just in the nick of time.

Again, he didn't need some high-priced shrink to point out that he had an overdeveloped Messiah complex that carried over into other areas of his life.

For all the good it did him. He had been helpless to save his mother, just as he was helpless to save Soqui. He was bad news for any woman stupid enough to let her life brush against his.

Especially Easton.

He rubbed a hand at the sudden ache in his chest. After a moment, he stepped away from the bed, satisfied that Belle was sound asleep.

He wasn't quite ready to go back to bed, so he walked to the window and pulled back the curtain. This room had basically the same view as his did next door—a view that had changed little since he lived here a few dozen lifetimes ago.

Same breathtaking soaring mountains, a vast black shadow in the moonlight, same comforting red-painted barn, same neat, straight fence lines. Being here in Cold Creek Canyon always managed to settle him somehow, to ease some nameless, restless ache he wasn't even aware of most of the time.

He loved the ranch, the only place he'd lived longer than a few weeks. Really, his first and only home.

When Jo and Guff first brought him here, he had been sure it was too good to last. Why would they want the skinny, smartass kid of a couple of migrant workers? He never expected to stay. In the back of his mind, he thought maybe with all the wide open spaces, he might have an easier time running away. He'd even stolen a tent out of the attic those first few days, just in case he had to escape into the mountains again.

He could still remember the day he arrived. Sure, he remembered Guff, who'd picked him up from the social worker's office in Idaho Falls. Tall and white-haired, his face leathery from years of working the land. And Jo, as skinny and petite as a kid, with snapping brown eyes and that wide, welcoming smile.

Yeah, he remembered the other boys. Quinn and Brant had both been here a while already and they were older and he'd been desperate for them to like him.

But mostly he remembered Easton. Blond braids flying under her little straw cowboy hat, the whitest, straightest teeth he'd ever seen, freckles across her soft, clean-scrubbed skin.

He had already lived twelve hard years on the planet and she was just about the prettiest thing he'd ever seen.

Nothing much had changed about that, after more than twenty years. She still was the most beautiful woman he knew, made even more lovely by her utter obliviousness to that fact.

Sometimes he wondered if it was the ranch that filled him with this sweet sense of peace or if it was Easton.

He let the curtain fall and turned back to the darkened nursery. Pain radiated from his wound. He could ignore it, but he knew it was going to keep him awake unless he took something for it. If he didn't sleep, he wouldn't be able to take care of Belle in the morning and he wasn't about to hand that responsibility off to Easton any more than he had to.

He had a bottle of pain pills on his bedside table, but he hated that woozy, not-quite-in-control feeling.

He would just grab a couple of ibuprofen, he decided. After a careful check at the crib to make sure Belle was still sleeping, he eased out into the dark hallway. A few more memories rushed back as he moved toward the stairs, other nights when he and Brant and Quinn had tried to sneak out for some mischief or other.

Quinn had usually been the ringleader, although Cisco had certainly contributed his share of lousy ideas. Brant, being the good, upstanding Dudley Do-Right that he still was, had usually tried like hell to talk them out of whatever trouble they were cooking up, but he rarely succeeded. The combined incendiary, seditious force of Quinn Southerland and Cisco del Norte was no match for somebody who always played by the rules.

Brant usually still came along, although Cisco had a feeling he was there more for damage control.

He moved gingerly down the stairs now, the damn

stitches Jake Dalton had stuck in him pulling with every step. Even so, he forgot about the tricky stair and winced when it squawked loudly in the still night.

That stupid stair had caused them no end of problems. He and Brant and Quinn had done their best to avoid it and had finally resorted to climbing out his bedroom window for their nocturnal wanderings.

Fat lot of good that did them. He smiled as he remembered one particular time they tried to sneak out for some midnight fishing on a school night. They had tried to sneak out his window—only to have the daylights scared out of them when Guff stepped out of the shadows by the old birch tree on the other side of the porch.

Cisco had only been at the ranch a few months at the time and he had been sure they were done for, but Guff had just grinned, loaded them up on horseback and taken them all up to the lake himself to show off his favorite fishing holes.

Jo had been ready to skin all of them the next morning when they showed up bleary-eyed for chores.

Ah, Guff. He missed the old codger.

Cisco had been in southern Mexico posing as a particularly repugnant low-level arms dealer when Jo finally reached out through channels to tell him his foster father had died. Even though it just about compromised the whole investigation, he had scrambled like hell to make it back in time for the funeral.

He closed his eyes, remembering the sorrow of those days, as intense as when his own father had died.

And after.

He didn't want to think about what happened after.

The house shifted and settled around him, its old bones creaking in the canyon winds.

This was a big house for one woman. Maybe Easton ought to think about leasing out the house and moving into the smaller foreman's house where she had lived with her parents.

He shoved thoughts of her away. Couldn't he go two seconds without her invading his mind, for heaven's sake?

In the kitchen, he opened the cabinet where Jo always kept a few first aid supplies. He pushed past bandages and aspirin and a tube of liniment. No ibuprofen. He pushed aside a roll of antacids when he suddenly heard a sound behind him, a shush of footsteps, the whisper of someone inhaling.

For a millisecond, he froze, then without even thinking—just acting completely on instinct—he whirled with the first weapon he could reach, the big deboning knife from the cutlery holder on the counter.

In a mortifying instant, he realized his mistake. Easton stood in the doorway wearing low-slung sleep pants and a short-cropped T-shirt, her hair tangled around her face.

Her gaze narrowed on the knife in his hand. "So far you've pulled a gun and a knife on me. What's next? Do you happen to have some C-4 in your pocket?"

He carefully set the knife back in the holder, angry at himself. "You're safe now," he said. From any weapons he might pull on her, anyway.

She walked into the kitchen and reached for a glass from the cabinet next to the sink. He tried not to notice how the thin material of her pajamas hugged her curves as she reached over her head.

After she filled her glass with water from the sink, she turned around, leaning a hip against the cabinet. "I'm curious about something."

In the low light above the stove, he could almost see her nipples through the thin material of her T-shirt. He quickly blinked and shifted his gaze, aghast at himself for looking.

"What are you curious about?" How he was going to keep her from noticing the sudden stir of interest below his waistband?

"Do you ever sleep? I mean, when you're living your life in whatever country you currently call home, doing whatever you do that you won't talk about?"

"I sleep."

"With a gun under your pillow and a knife at your side?"

Sometimes. And sometimes even those safeguards were still flimsy protection.

His best option was to ignore her questions, he decided. His sole objective these last few years when it came to Easton Springhill was to keep the ugliness of his life from oozing into hers.

"I came down looking for ibuprofen. You have any?"

She set down her water glass. In her eyes, he could see she knew quite well he was trying to distract her and had decided to let him.

"The pain pills Jake gave you aren't cutting it?"

"Didn't take any today," he admitted. "I figured I'd start with vitamin I and see if I need anything stronger."

She gave him a long look and he could tell she had plenty she wanted to say to him, but to his relief she finally shrugged and reached into a drawer. She tossed the bottle toward him and he caught it one-handed. By the time he unscrewed the top and popped some out, she had poured him another glass of water.

"Thanks."

She raised an eyebrow at the four pills in his hand but made no comment.

"I'm sorry I woke you," he said after he'd taken the pills. "I forgot about the squeaky step."

She smiled a little at that and he was struck again by how lovely she was, how perfect she had felt in his arms.

"Sometimes I think Guff might have done something to the wood on that particular step when he was building the house, just as a precautionary alarm," she said. "He caught me a few times in high school."

"Why, Easton Springhill, you naughty thing. I had no idea. Where were you going?"

She gave him a sidelong look. "Not where you think. I was a good girl, unlike you boys. Usually I just needed a midnight ride."

"Except for those times you snuck out to be with us."

She made a rueful face. "Well, except for that. Do you remember that time I begged you guys to take me riding with you to Hidden Falls? I was maybe thirteen and my mom said I was getting too old for overnight trips with you guys. I was crushed."

"I remember." That was one of the times Guff hadn't been as forgiving, after they sneaked Easton out of her house and left only a note for her mother letting her know when they would be back.

He could still remember the long lecture Guff had

given them all, his stern reminder that East wasn't a little girl anymore and like all young ladies, she needed to be treated with respect for her reputation.

"We were a bad influence on an innocent little girl, always dragging you into trouble of some kind or another."

She raised an eyebrow. "And what's changed?"

He thought of Belle sleeping upstairs and all the complications his presence here had caused for Easton.

"Your mom and dad should have locked you up the moment Jo and Guff brought Quinn onto the ranch. We really were a bad influence on you."

She was quiet for a moment as the refrigerator compressor hummed to life. Finally, one corner of her mouth lifted in a half smile. "My life was far richer for the three of you. Brant and Quinn were the older brothers I always dreamed of and you were, well…" Her voice trailed off.

"I was what?" he asked, despite his instincts that were urging him to get the hell out of the kitchen right now, especially with his control teetering on a razor's edge.

"Not a brother. I would think that's obvious," she murmured.

He let out a breath and stepped closer to her, ignoring the strident warning bell in his head. He couldn't seem to help himself, driven by the low throb of desire that had been humming through him since she walked into the kitchen.

Her gaze flashed to his and her eyes widened. He saw awareness flicker there, saw her breath catch. She swallowed hard, her hand tightly clutching her water glass.

Not a good idea to act on lesser impulses when he was tired and hurting and not completely in control of himself. Better to just walk away now, before he caused even more trouble in her life.

He might have done just that, but then he thought he saw something deep in her eyes, a hunger there that matched his own.

"Cisco—"

Whatever she intended to say was lost, swallowed up by his mouth brushing against hers.

Heaven.

Her mouth was cool from the water glass and she tasted minty and sweet. Her breath caught between them and her skin smelled sleepy and sexy, of wildflowers and warm, luscious female.

During his darkest moments when he was so tangled in a job he couldn't always figure out where his cover ended and he began, he would cling to the memory of Easton's kisses, of those stolen moments in the shelter he and Quinn and Brant had built on the shore of Windy Lake.

The unexpected delight of having her in his arms, the vague sense of wonder to find her kissing him back. The desperate heat, underscored by their shared grief for her uncle, his foster father.

He remembered every moment of their time together five years ago. Each sigh, each gasp. The angle of her head as he touched her, the flutter of her hands curling into his shirt. The agonizingly sweet welcome of her body.

This, though, the sheer delicious reality of having her in his arms once more—of her heat and softness against his skin, of her mouth trembling beneath his—beat the echo of those memories all to hell.

He knew it wouldn't last. It couldn't. In a moment, one or both of them would find a semblance of good sense and pull away. But for now, she was here in his arms and she was kissing him and the prowling restlessness inside him quieted.

She clung to him, her small, capable hands wrapped around his bare waist. He pressed her back against the edge of the kitchen table. Either those ibuprofen tablets were sheer magic or she was one powerful distraction because he forgot all about the aches and pains that had left him weak and miserable for the last two days.

All he could think about was Easton. When it came right down to it, she was the only thing in his life that mattered.

"Cisco."

Just that. His name.

The sound of it was at once unbearably erotic and the harsh slap of reality he'd been half expecting.

He couldn't do this. Not here, not with her.

Things were tense enough between them and had been for the last five years. He knew he was to blame. He lived with that knowledge, along with his memories. He was a bastard who had allowed his feelings to roar out of control five years ago, who had completely taken advantage of her vulnerability and their shared grief over Guff's death.

She had been a virgin. Twenty-four years old and she'd never been with anyone else. He still hated himself for taking that from her and for the pitiful little part of him that still found a primitive, macho satisfaction in that.

Nothing had been the same since that fateful night. The next day, he had returned to the job, to slogging his way through the grime and the muck, a world away from Winder Ranch and Easton.

Three months later, a letter from Jo had been passed to him by his handler. He'd been recovering again, this time from the gunshot wound from that stupid little rebel soldier with the uncharacteristically accurate aim.

Jo had mentioned, almost in passing, that Easton was taking a job with a cattleman's association in Denver and leaving Winder Ranch.

Because of him.

His foster mother hadn't needed to spell it out for him to understand. Not that Jo knew anything. He sensed she might have suspected something had happened between them after Guff's funeral, but she'd never outright asked him.

But he knew, even if Jo hadn't, that Easton must have been so upset with him for taking advantage of her that she was willing to leave everything she loved, even the still-grieving Jo, so she wouldn't have to see him again.

He had tried to stay away as long as he could, but eighteen months later he couldn't avoid it. Quinn tracked him down to tell him he was throwing a surprise birthday party for Jo and if Cisco didn't find a way to make it, Quinn would fly down to whatever hellhole he currently called home and drag him back by his scrawny little neck.

He had managed to squeeze out a few days to go home. By then, Easton had moved back to Winder

Ranch, apparently finished with her short-lived thirst for adventure beyond Pine Gulch.

Cisco had been stunned by the differences in her. She had been quiet, pale. Had barely looked him in the eye.

In the three years since, little had changed. Her eyes still turned that murky blue when she looked at him, she still flinched whenever he touched her.

Except now. He frowned. This was a fluke, he told himself. She must be as tired as he was. That still didn't make it a good idea.

Though it took every ounce of will, he forced himself to slide his mouth away and step back a pace.

Her eyes fluttered open and she stared at him, though he couldn't read her emotions in her eyes. She used to be so open, exuberant with happiness, tender-hearted toward anyone in need. Over the years, she had become adept at hiding herself away.

"If Quinn or Brant were here, they would probably warn you in their capacity as the protective big brothers you never had that you really ought to stay away from dark rooms in the middle of the night with men who aren't fully in control of themselves. I'm sorry, Easton."

After a long moment, her expression turned chilly and finally he could clearly read the emotion there—she was supremely pissed.

"Since they're not here, I'm sure they would appreciate you stepping in with your wise advice. Next time, maybe you ought to think about pulling that out first instead of a carving knife or a .45."

It was a 9 mm, but he decided this probably wasn't the best time to correct her.

"I'm going back to bed," she said.

"Don't worry about Belle in the morning. I should be able to handle things from here on out. Thank you for everything you've done the last few days."

She gave him another cool look, then turned from the kitchen, leaving him alone with his guilt and his memories.

Chapter Five

Few things could match the sheer breathtaking beauty of a Cold Creek morning in late spring.

The sun hadn't come up yet, though the mountains to the east wore a pale blue rim. The predawn air was cool but not cold enough for frost. Here in the mountains above the ranch, everything smelled sweet and pure, a delicious mix of sage and pine and new springtime growth. Add to that the distinctive scents of leather tack and horse and she was in heaven.

Jack, her best cow dog, ran ahead on the trail, sniffing at squirrel scents or bugs or who knew what else.

She loved these morning rides, even with this little twinge of guilt that had settled on her shoulders.

She didn't really have time for a pleasure ride this morning. Despite Cisco's last words to her the night before, she knew Belle would be waking soon and she wasn't sure she felt comfortable leaving her with a man who had been out of his head twenty-four hours ago with fever.

On the other hand, he had somehow summoned enough energy to kiss her senseless, so he was right that he could probably handle the baby for a while.

This was ranch business anyway, she told herself. Burt had e-mailed her—his new favorite form of communication since his daughter bought him a netbook for Christmas—that the creek was running high up on one of the high pastures and he was worried about it flooding the nearby hay shed.

She thought she might be able to sneak away to check out the situation and return to the ranch before the baby even awoke.

Besides, it wasn't as if she could sleep anyway, not after her encounter with Cisco in the kitchen. She sighed and tried to push the memory away. Better to focus on the beauty of the morning, of the strong horse beneath her and her dog's happy snuffling.

The mountains around the ranch gave peace to her spirit. They always had. When she had come back to Pine Gulch and Winder Ranch five years ago, she had been lost, scoured raw with grief. The depth of her pain seemed unfathomable, so vast and all-encompassing she had been certain it would pull her under.

She hadn't told anyone, not even Jo, though she was almost certain her aunt had suspected something about what had happened in the year since Uncle Guff died. Jo had welcomed her back to Winder Ranch without asking questions. Easton had always adored her aunt, but Jo's gentle love, her unfailing acceptance, during that time had been exactly what she needed.

Easton had thrown herself into running the ranch,

learning all she could in preparation for taking over for Jo one day.

She had soaked in all the advice her aunt had to offer, every bit of guidance from Burt, even the half-joking tips from the old codgers who hung out at the café in town shooting the shinola, as Guff used to say.

And then only a year after her return, Jo had first been diagnosed with cancer and Easton's thirst for ranch knowledge had become insatiable.

For the next three years as Jo fought her illness, more of the responsibility for the ranch had fallen on Easton. She hadn't minded. She loved the land, the changing seasons, the thrill and the challenge of it.

No matter what she was going through, she had turned to the mountains when her spirit was troubled or worn down.

Like now. Coming to check on the hay shed had only been an excuse. She could have done it later in the day or even tomorrow since Burt had assured her the creek had a few days before it crested. She also could have taken a pickup and driven on the dirt road on the other side of the foothill, which would have made for a much shorter excursion.

She had other reasons for wanting to be on Lucky Star instead of a pickup. She needed the comfort and routine she found on horseback and she had to admit, it was working. She certainly felt better now than she had since the early hours of the morning when she had left Cisco's arms.

She almost thought she might be able to make it through the rest of the day with him there at the ranch house.

"Almost," she said aloud, and Lucky's ears flickered.

Jack yapped agreement and Easton smiled as the first rays of the sun peeked over the mountain.

After checking out the flooding situation, she paused a moment to appreciate the morning, then decided she had dawdled enough. She turned her horse around and was heading down the hill toward the ranch house when the jittery bleat of her cell phone shattered the quiet morning peace.

Jack barked in response, while Easton fumbled in her pocket of her denim jacket for two more rings before her fingers finally closed around the dratted thing. She assumed Burt was trying to reach her to make a decision about something, but to her considerable surprise, the number on the caller ID display was someone else entirely.

"Mimi!" she exclaimed when she answered the call. "What are you doing up so early? I can't imagine the sun is even up in L.A.! It's barely daylight here."

Mimi van Hoyt Western—spoiled society heiress, adoring wife, mother of one of the most darling little girls on the planet, and one of Easton's closest friends— gave a rueful chuckle. "Brant had to report at 0500 for a training mission, so of course Abby and I had to wake up to see him off. Well, I woke up to see him off and Abby woke up because she's teething. As a bonus, she got to say bye to her daddy."

Nearly eighteen months ago, Mimi had driven her car into the creek on Brant's family ranch during a February blizzard. Much to everyone's surprise, an unlikely romance began between her quiet, solemn war hero of a friend and the tabloid princess—who happened to be pregnant with another man's baby at the time.

They married last August, just in time for Abby's

arrival. Easton couldn't be more delighted that Brant found someone so perfect for him. Mimi's fun-loving, light-hearted assault on life was the perfect foil to the serious, dedicated Army major who always tried to do the right thing.

After several long deployments to the Middle East, Brant had been stationed stateside for the past six months, much to Easton's relief.

"What are you up to?" Mimi asked now.

"Enjoying a spectacular sunrise on the Windy Lake trail," she answered. "I wish you could see it."

"I do, too. Take a picture with your phone and e-mail me," Mimi ordered, in that peremptory way of hers that somehow always came across charming instead of bossy. "But I didn't mean what are you up to right this moment in time. It was more a question in the global sense."

"In what way?" she stalled, though she had a feeling she could guess where this was going.

"We're hearing rumors about you."

"Wow. Clear in Los Angeles? I would have figured you just have to look out your window to find people doing far more interesting things than I."

"True enough. The other day, you wouldn't believe what I saw outside Pinkberry. But I digress. Tess called me last night from Seattle with some interesting gossip about you, but we figured it was too late for either of us to call you for verification."

Easton winced. She should have expected this. Brant and Quinn weren't the only overprotective ones in her little family.

"Mimi, I'm shocked. You, of all people, know you shouldn't believe every interesting bit of gossip you hear, right? For instance, I read in a fairly reliable magazine at the supermarket checkout that you were pregnant again, with quintuplets this time. Guess Brant must have some serious warrior sperm. Or it was possibly an alien abduction sort of thing."

Mimi laughed. "Shut it, you. I'm not pregnant. Maybe in a year or two and not quintuplets, God willing. But we're not talking about me or any silly tabloid. Tess heard Cisco is in town."

She grimaced, grateful Mimi couldn't see her. She really didn't want to get into this right now.

"Just what sort of spy network do the two of you have since you both live hundreds of miles away?"

"Well, Tess's mother was at the florist in Pine Gulch when she could swear she saw you and Cisco come out of the clinic across the street. And get this, she has some crazy notion that you had a baby with you. I told Tess maybe her mother stopped off at The Gulch for a few too many appletinis on her way to the florist. Or maybe she needs to get a new eyeglass prescription."

Easton let out an exasperated breath. "Do they even serve appletinis at The Gulch?"

"No idea. I say we go find out next time I'm in town since I'm not nursing anymore. But again, not the point. Is Cisco there?"

She sighed. "It is completely impossible to keep anything secret in Pine Gulch. I should know that by now."

Except one thing. Her hands tightened on the reins at the grim thought. Somehow, against all conceivable odds, she had managed to conceal one salient detail about her life from everyone in Cold Creek.

Especially from Cisco.

"So it's true?"

"Yes, it's true. Mrs. Jamison doesn't miss a trick. You should know that. You can assure Tess her mother hasn't been drinking and she doesn't need new glasses. Cisco showed up here two days ago."

Mimi was quiet for a long moment and Easton could almost hear her speculation in the silence. She strongly suspected Mimi and Tess both had guessed her feelings for Cisco to some degree, though neither woman had ever pressed her on it.

"So are you going to explain or leave me hanging here? Why is he back? Where has he been? Why were you at the medical clinic? And for heaven's sake, where does the baby come in?"

She laughed at the barrage of questions, grateful to Mimi for diverting her from her lingering malaise after the kiss.

"The baby is an orphan from Colombia whose father apparently had family here, so she has dual citizenship. He's trying to transfer custody to an aunt, who won't be available to take her for a few more days."

"And why is Cisco involved in this? Is he in the adoption business these days?"

"I guess he was friends with both parents. The mother's last wish was for the baby to come back to the U.S."

"So the baby isn't his?"

"Apparently not."

"And the clinic? What was that about? Is everybody okay?"

"Geez, Mimi. You haven't even asked what I'm wearing yet. And don't you want to know what I'm planning to fix for breakfast this morning?"

The other woman laughed. "I figured you would rather get the third degree from me instead of my highly trained special forces soldier of a husband. Consider it a favor. You know I'm just being nosy so you won't have to go through all this with Brant, who happens to be much better at interrogation than I am."

"I think you can probably give him a run for his money," Easton muttered as she reached the barn.

"So why were you there? Is the baby sick?"

She dismounted, her phone still nestled in the crook of her shoulder as she began to work the surcingle.

"Not the baby." She paused, wondering how much she should share with Mimi. Finally she opted for honesty. With their intricate intelligence network, Mimi and Tess would find out soon enough.

"I had to take Cisco in to see Jake. He's came home with a knife wound that's become infected. But don't worry, Jake's on top of things."

"He always is," Mimi said with obvious fondness for the doctor who had delivered her baby. "Good grief, though. A knife wound?"

"I know, right."

"That man. I'd like to give him a good, hard shake. Doesn't he know how much you all worry about him while he's living so hard down there?"

"He knows."

The man would have to be an idiot not to know—and Cisco was many things but he wasn't stupid.

"To be honest, I'm not so sure it matters much to him or he would have come back years ago."

Mimi made a sound of disgust that still managed to come across as elegant. "I worry enough about Brant," she said. "It's one thing for him to put himself in harm's way. But he's an Army Ranger and that's what he signed up for. Those of us who love him have to just accept that this is his particular calling. But none of us knows *what* Cisco is up to down there. I think that's what makes Brant the most crazy."

"Yeah, me, too."

Mimi's voice softened. "Having him there can't be easy for you, can it? How are you holding up, honey?"

Again, she winced at the mingled concern and speculation in the words.

"No big deal." She tried for a casual tone but she was pretty sure the effort fell flat. "You know I'm always happy when any of the family can make it home."

"Do you want me and Abby to come out there? Brant's going to be gone for two weeks on this assignment, so our schedule is pretty free, except for a command performance at Grandpa's."

Mimi's father, Werner van Hoyt, was a brash, powerful Hollywood producer and real estate mogul who had completely shocked Mimi by embracing his role in his beloved granddaughter's life.

Easton considered having Mimi and Abby there. She supposed they would provide a much-needed buffer between her and Cisco, perhaps ease some of the awkwardness. It was difficult for anyone to be stiff and uncomfortable with Mimi around and Abby completely charmed anyone who wandered into her orbit.

On the other hand, Easton didn't want to drag her friend and her teething baby across several state lines—and some silly part of her wanted to selfishly hoard this rare time with Cisco.

"We'll be fine. I'm sure he won't be here for long, once Belle is settled. You know how Cisco is."

"That man," Mimi said again. "Someone ought to glue his shoes to the floor to keep him where he belongs."

"Yeah, but they'd have to catch him first and he's a slippery one."

Mimi gave a short laugh. "True enough. Well, you be careful. If you change your mind about Abby and me coming out, let me know."

"I will."

After they said their goodbyes, Easton finished removing the horse's tack and let her out to pasture.

Easton watched Lucky roll in the spring grasses for a moment before she climbed up and headed to the water trough.

Be careful, Mimi had said.

Easton supposed that meant she ought to try avoiding any more midnight trips to the kitchen, especially if she might encounter any dangerous men so hopped up on ibuprofen they can't control themselves around her.

She sighed. If she could only stay up the mountains until he was gone, everything would be fine. Too bad for her, that was impossible.

"Hold still, sugar, or we're both going to make a mess here."

Belle giggled and clapped her hands while Cisco struggled to pull the front part of the diaper over her and fasten the tabs around her chubby little legs.

Diapering a baby definitely wasn't part of his skill set. He'd come to that rather grim conclusion the first day after Soqui died. He wanted to think he'd become a little better at it with all the practice he'd had the last week, but not much. His hands had never felt so big, his fingers so ungainly.

"Almost done with the diaper. Then on to the clothes."

She twisted her body, reaching over her head for the box of wipes he'd set at the head of the changing table.

"Hey, hold still, you." He quickly handed her a stuffed dog with an assortment of sensory offerings for paws. A squeaker in one leg, something crinkly and noisy in the other, a couple of nubby teething rings.

What a blessing that for the most part she was a happy, easygoing little kid. He could tell she missed her mama and couldn't quite understand why her circumstances had changed so dramatically. Sometimes she would cry pitifully for a few moments, but she could always be cajoled out of a major tantrum.

She seemed to have adapted with remarkable ease to having a fumbling, inept bachelor caretaking her.

He could only keep his fingers crossed that she continued this whole easygoing routine. "You've got to make a good impression on your auntie tomorrow, kiddo," he told her now and Belle blew a raspberry at him and gnawed on her puppy.

He sure hoped he'd done the right thing, bringing her here and setting her up to live with a stranger. Yeah, he was only following what Soqui had begged him to do as she lay dying. But ultimately, no matter her mother's wishes, he was still responsible.

Too late to change things now, he supposed. The

wheels were in motion and Belle's aunt would arrive at the ranch the next day to pick her up.

He wasn't entirely sure how he felt about that, if he were honest with himself. Belle was a cute little thing and he would miss her, he supposed.

"It's for the best," he assured her as he finished pulling on her little pink sweatpants and went to work on her socks.

"Gaaaaa," she expounded.

"My sentiments exactly," he said.

She grinned at him, that big gummy smile that showed off her two little pearly whites. "Babababababababa."

"You said it, sister."

A low laugh rippled through the room and he jerked his gaze to the doorway. Easton stood with one hip against the jamb, her arms crossed over her chest. Her cheeks were slightly pink from being outside and her sleek waterfall of blond hair was braided down her back. She looked sweet and fresh and innocent and so lovely it made his throat ache.

How long had she been there? He tried to tell himself the heat soaking his face was probably just a few lingering remnants of fever.

She quickly transformed her laugh into a cough. "Don't stop on my account. Sounded like the two of you were solving the world's problems."

"We're finished. Aren't we, *bellissima?*"

The baby gurgled her agreement and handed him the slobbery stuffed dog.

"Um. Thanks."

He slanted a look at Easton and found her watching him, an intense, unreadable look in her eyes.

After a moment, she blinked and looked away. "I'm

really sorry. I didn't realize Belle would wake so early or I wouldn't have left the house. I had to check a few things up in the high pasture, but I thought I could be back before either of you were up."

"We're not your responsibility. I told you I could handle things with her today."

"Everything on the ranch is my responsibility," she said simply.

She loved the ranch. She always had. When she wasn't chasing after Quinn, Brant and him, she was following her father. Easton had never been happier than when she was doing ranchwork. Didn't matter what— working on the insides of a tractor with Quinn, moving irrigation sprinkler pipe or on the back of a horse having a contest with him to see who could round up more strays in their grazing allotment.

She belonged in this place. The rest of them had wandered away, like the Four Winds Jo used to call them because of their directional names. Quinn Southerland settled in Seattle, where he ran a wildly successful transportation company. Brant Western had joined the Army the moment he could and had quickly been channeled through officer training. Since then, he'd served overseas more times than he'd been stateside.

And Cisco. Well, he had wandered plenty for all of them.

"How is she doing today? Did she sleep well?"

He shrugged. "She woke up an hour ago a bit on the cranky side. I think she was missing her mama."

He regretted the word the moment he said it. Belle pulled the dog's ear away from her mouth and looked around the room as if expecting Soqui to show up any moment. When nobody else materialized, Belle's little chin started quivering.

"Maamaaamaaamaaaa," she whimpered.

Easton's blue eyes filled with a deep sympathy. "Poor little lamb."

Although he was still holding the baby, Easton leaned in and pressed a kiss to the top of Isabella's tousled curls.

She smelled deliciously of spring, of wildflowers and rainshowers. His body stirred, caught up in memories of slender curves and soft skin and the tiny, sexy sounds she made when he kissed her.

"My heart just breaks for her," she said.

Easton had always been so tender-hearted toward anybody—or anything—in pain. The scrawniest calves, baby birds that fell out of the nest, the kid on the schoolbus that no one else sat by.

Even him.

After Guff's death, he had been in a dark, ugly place, knowing that this man he respected and loved so much had died believing Cisco was a useless ne'er-do-well with nothing on his mind but tequila and women.

Easton had reached out to him. She had followed him into the mountains after the funeral when he had been desperate for escape. She had kissed him because she felt sorry for him and he, in his supreme selfishness, had taken things too far.

"She'll be okay. Some part of her will always miss her mama, I imagine."

"Like you?"

He flashed her a quick look. "And you. I was only three when I lost my mother. You had a lot more years and memories to get past."

"The absence is the same, no matter your age," she answered quietly. "You and I were both blessed to have Jo to fill the void a little. I hope Belle's aunt will step up and be the mother she needs."

John's sister had sounded nice enough on the phone, though decidedly frazzled. He couldn't blame her, since she had been making her father's funeral arrangements at the time. Cisco just had to hope she didn't turn out to be some cranky hag who hated kids.

"I hope so. There. Now you're all ready for breakfast?" he said to Belle, who giggled and gnawed the dog a little harder.

"May I take her?" Easton asked.

"Sure."

She pulled the baby into her arms and Cisco told himself that ache in his gut as he watched Easton press her cheek to Belle's was only a little hunger pang.

"How are you feeling?" she asked as she led the way down the stairs toward the kitchen. "Any more fever?"

Only for you.

He forced himself to shrug. "The antibiotics Jake gave me seem to have kicked in. I'm fine now. Great."

It wasn't exactly the truth, but he wasn't about to tell her he still felt like three-day-old roadkill.

Her eyebrows raised skeptically, but before she could call him the liar that he undoubtedly was, he opted to distract her.

"What was the crisis that had you out so early?"

"Not really a crisis." In a matter of seconds, she competently buckled Belle into the high chair in the kitchen, when it had taken him a good ten minutes to figure out the complicated rigging the night before.

"We're having some runoff issues," she went on. "You know how it is in the springtime. The creek's running high this year from the heavy snows we had over the winter, and I told Burt I would go up to take a look and see if we need to sandbag the hay shed up there in the upper pasture."

He poured coffee. "Do you?"

"The creek will be cresting in the next day or so and my gut is saying the water won't go high enough to reach the hay."

"But you're going to have Burt and the boys sandbag anyway," he guessed.

She flashed him a rueful smile. "Of course."

"Was it Guff or Jo who used to always remind us it wasn't raining when Noah built the ark?"

She laughed. "Both, I think. And my father, too. When you fail to prepare, you should prepare to fail, right? I had it drilled into me from the time I was Belle's age, I think."

After a moment, his answering smile slid away. "This is a bad time for me to show up with another complication, isn't it?"

She avoided his gaze and sipped at her own coffee. "You know how it is around here," she finally said. "When could you find a good time?"

"I don't know. Maybe November twenty-first for roughly a three-hour window."

She laughed. "Make it two and you might have a deal."

There wasn't really a slow season on an Idaho cattle ranch. He knew that well. Winter was long and hard and usually bitter cold and busy since they calved in late January. Spring was planting season, a time of growth and new life. Summer meant moving the cattle to the high-country grazing range, when the nights were crisp but the days were glorious. Fall, of course, meant the crop harvest and rounding up the cattle and taking them to market. Hectic and crazy and fun.

The steady rhythm of it had been a wonder and a comfort to a kid who had spent so much of his life in uncertainty.

When he first came to the ranch, he hadn't known how to handle staying in one place for longer than a few weeks at a time. Winter had completely freaked him out. Migrant farmworkers and their families tended not to have a lot of experience with snow, since they usually moved on when the harvest is over.

Here he had found a home. Jo and Guff had opened their hearts and their lives to him and he never forgot what a blessing that had been.

He had come to love them both—and Quinn and Brant, whom he considered brothers in every possible way.

None of them had it easy before they came to the ranch. When Quinn moved in with the Winders, he had been angry and bitter and had taken a long time to deal with the murder-suicide of his parents. He hadn't trusted anyone and had been certain the Winders would betray him, just like everyone close to him had done.

Brant had turned inward and become even more serious and dependable as he worked to prove to everyone in town he wasn't his deadbeat, abusive father.

As for Cisco, he had become adept at pretending to become whatever anybody else needed him to be.

A chameleon. With Jo and Guff, he was grateful, hardworking, eager to please. At school, he had charmed all the teachers with his ready smile and quick wit. He'd had plenty of friends because he was always coming up with new, exciting schemes to break the monotony of school and the quiet steadiness of life in a small town.

He had loved Winder Ranch and the people around Cold Creek Canyon and would forever be grateful for the turn his life had taken when the Winders offered him a home.

Without Jo and Guff, he probably would have turned to drugs like so many other troubled kids did and then a life of crime to support his habit.

Not that what he did now was so very different.

He hadn't realized he had sighed until Easton touched his shoulder, then quickly moved her hand away. "You're hurting, aren't you?"

"Why would you say that?" He did his best to ignore the sparks that brief, comforting touch sent coursing through him.

"You always get this distant sort of look in your eyes when you're trying to hide your emotions."

"Do I?" he asked, surprised. He had a reputation for coolness, even callousness. Could she really see through the mask?

She sipped at her own coffee. "Everybody always thought you were so cheerful all the time. Always laughing, playing pranks, always up for the next joke. But I could tell when it was just an act."

He didn't want to think about just how her insight into his psyche had always terrified him.

"In this case, you're wrong. I'm really fine," he lied. "Is there something Belle and I can help you do around the ranch today to help pay for our room and board?"

She frowned. "Sure. I've got a great idea. Why don't you go back to bed and let me take care of Belle?"

He ignored her suggestion. "Any errands you need run in town? Anything we could pick up at the feed store for you? I'm pretty sure I can still work a tractor, though it's been a few years. I can put her in her car seat and take her along."

"Do you really think I would send you out to drive heavy farm machinery in your condition? Jake told me to make sure you take it easy for the next few days and that's just what you're going to do."

"I don't need a babysitter, Easton."

"Are you sure about that?" Her stare turned as cold as Winder Lake in January. "How many thirty-three-year-old men are still running around getting in bar fights in some greasy Colombian cantina?"

"Only the lucky few." He tried for an insouciant smile, although it was difficult. He knew he shouldn't allow her obviously poor opinion of him to sting like a hundred hornets. It was his own fault she had that view of him, one he had cultivated for the last decade, of a shiftless wanderer.

He could always tell her the truth about his injury, about Soqui's death, about what he was really doing when he left the ranch. But he had been warned early in the game by more than one agent to keep those he cared about out of the loop about his activities, for their own protection. John and Soqui were perfect examples. John had let Soqui into their dark and twisted world and she had died as a result.

Since Easton topped the list of people he cared about, he just had to endure her poor opinion and let it wash over him.

This time didn't seem as easy as usual and apparently she wasn't done gouging out his heart.

"When are you going to finally grow up, Cisco?" Even though her words were harsh, her voice was soft and sad. "Why don't you do something real with your life instead of working whatever schemes you're doing down there?"

He couldn't do this. Not today, after he had held her sweetness in his arms in the night, when his defenses were already dangerously thin.

"Back off, East."

She ignored him as he suspected she would. "Come home, Cisco. For good this time, I mean."

He stared. "Here?"

Color rose on her cheeks. "Not necessarily here. You know what I mean. I'm sure Quinn could find you a job somewhere at Southerland Shipping up in Seattle."

What the hell was he qualified for, after a decade of secrets and subterfuge? Working as some clerk for his best friend?

"I don't think so," he answered, then added another lie. "I'm living the dream."

"But how can you possibly be happy with that sort of life? Always moving from place to place. On the run all the time."

He supposed the irony of the whole thing was that when he was a kid, all he had ever wanted was a place to call home. He could remember lying in the grass on the edge of a vast cherry orchard, talking to another kid of a migrant worker, telling him the first thing he would do when he had saved enough money from the three dollars a crate they were paid was buy a house of his own. Some place where he could park an old car in the garage and fix it up sweet, where he could sit on the back porch and drink beer in the evening, where he could have a pretty woman in the kitchen making him tamales whenever he wanted.

Yeah, he'd been a serious chauvinist when he was ten. But it had seemed like everything he could ever want.

And now his life was not unlike his father's, only he wasn't harvesting crops. He was on some misguided quest to save the damn world.

"I don't know what you're doing down there," Easton said. "But it surely can't be too late to make a clean start. I know you, Cisco. I know you can't be happy."

"You don't know me. Not anymore." He flung the bitter words at her and he thought her skin turned a shade paler.

"Obviously not," she said, her voice low. "But I do know you broke Jo's heart over and over before she died. Do you have any idea how much she worried about you all the time? And so do I."

"Don't waste your time or energy. Nobody asked you to be my frigging conscience," he snapped, his voice so harsh that the baby started to fret.

Easton glared. "Now look. You've upset Belle."

Of course he had. Because he was an irresponsible idiot who spent his days drinking and carousing with the *chicas* and otherwise squandering his life away.

He ignored the pain of her poor opinion and turned his attention to the baby. "Hush, sweetheart. Easy."

He crooned to her in Spanish, the songs imprinted on his memory by another woman he had failed.

Belle didn't care if he was disappointing everyone in his life. He supposed that was one of the beautiful things about children. They loved you without judgment or expectations, except that you send that love right back at them.

When he looked up, Easton was watching with that tight, unreadable expression again. "You seem to have everything under control here," she said stiffly. "Since you don't need anything from me, I have work to do."

He thought about telling her. There would be some grim satisfaction in it, he supposed. *Hey, funny thing. I'm not running from the law. I* am *the law. How about that? I've been an undercover drug agent since I was recruited a decade ago fresh out of the Marines.*

But the truth was, she was better off thinking the worst of him. How could he let her down if she didn't expect anything of him? He was already as low in her esteem as he could get, so he couldn't disappoint her more.

His mother, Soqui. Even little Belle.

Any female who brushed up against his world ended up paying dearly for her mistakes and he couldn't do that to Easton.

Chapter Six

She managed to avoid the house for the rest of the morning, even though she was ashamed at her own weakness.

She should be tough enough to face him. She had offered her advice, had urged him to come back and settle down. If he chose a different path, she couldn't do anything about it. What did she accomplish by rushing away to sulk? Absolutely nothing.

Burt hadn't been expecting her help today since she had told him she expected to be busy at the house with Belle all day. As a result, she spent the morning with busy work. Cleaning out the stalls, fixing a few loose fence rails, organizing the tack room.

Finally she had run out of make-work and had turned her attention to Jo's vegetable garden.

She supposed it could still be called a garden, though only barely. After two summers of virtual neglect by

Easton, the garden was in pretty sorry shape, weedy and overgrown. She had hours of hard, sweaty work ahead of her clearing out the weeds and spading in some soil prep so she could plant a few tomato plants for August beefsteaks.

Yanking weeds and attacking the garden mess was slow and monotonous, something that kept her hands busy but left her mind entirely too free to wander through the muck, into things she didn't want to think about.

Suzy brought her pups out to enjoy the May sunshine and Easton paused to watch them chase each other around the bench where Jo used to love to sit and raise her face to the sun.

She shouldn't have said anything to Cisco. The way he lived his life wasn't any of her business. Hadn't he made that clear enough over the years?

When he first took off down south after a short stint in the Marines, Easton thought maybe he was just trying to connect with the part of his past, his heritage, that had died with his father. But when those first months had stretched into a year and then two with no sign that he wanted to come home, no fixed address they could contact him at, no apparent direction or legitimate source of income, she had been consumed with worry.

Jo and Guff had worried, too. She knew they had. But whenever he would come home, Cisco would smile and joke and charm them all into believing he would be okay.

Over the years, the laughter had faded from those dark eyes. That's what she hated the most.

Once, after he hadn't called home for eight or nine

months, Jo had sat her down and reminded her Cisco was an adult, free to make his own choices.

"What if his choices are stupid?" Easton had retorted.

"Then he will hopefully learn not to make the same stupid choices the next time," Jo had answered in that calm, no-nonsense voice of hers. "All we can do is pray and cry a little bit for him and be here waiting for him when he decides to come home."

Easton had waited. Those first few years after he left, she had missed him terribly—and his infrequent phone calls and e-mails would leave her more worried than ever but still praying for the next one.

She was pathetic. She knew it. After Guff died, when everything changed, she had dreaded that occasional contact, unable to bear her worry for him.

She shoved Jo's favorite shovel into a particularly nasty rush skeleton weed, grunting at the effort.

Gardening wasn't necessarily her favorite activity, but she had to admit she found a deep sense of accomplishment when she was able to work the spindly thing free of the soil to toss into the wheelbarrow.

One of Suzy's pups wandered over and pulled out the weed. He shook it back and forth as if it were a deadly enemy.

"Hey, quit it, you. You're going to spread nasty noxious seeds all over my garden."

The puppy barked at her and scampered away, the weed still in its mouth. She chased after it across the grass, laughing despite her lingering frustration with Cisco. Just before she caught up, she heard the crunch of tires on the long gravel drive that led to Cold Creek Canyon Road.

She finally wrenched the weed away from Suzy's pup and tossed a twig for it instead, then shaded her eyes with her hand. When the vehicle drew closer, she recognized the blue-and-white Pine Gulch police department SUV.

Easton set her hoe against the garden fence and walked through the gate toward the driveway, just as the vehicle pulled to a stop. A moment later, Trace Bowman opened the door of his vehicle and climbed out.

He raised a hand in greeting when he saw her and took off his dark sunglasses, shoving them in his pocket as he walked along the path toward her.

He really was remarkably good-looking, with that sun-streaked brown hair and that edge of clean-cut, heroic earnestness about him.

She wanted so desperately to feel something for him. If she loved Trace Bowman, he wouldn't break her heart again and again.

"Something wrong, Officer? I could swear I wasn't speeding. In fact, I do believe I'm the slowest weeder in the county."

His smile glinted in the sunlight. "Nothing wrong. I had some business out this way and figured I would stop in and check on things since I was in the neighborhood."

He was great-looking, nice and cared about her well-being. Why couldn't she have the good sense to relish those things? Instead, she was like Suzy's fat little pup, determined to go after the one thing that wasn't good for her.

"Did del Norte take off again?" Trace asked, scanning the area with what she guessed was a practiced lawman's eye.

"Not yet. The, um, baby's aunt had a funeral in Montana, so she was delayed. She's going to pick Belle up on her way back to Boise either tomorrow or the next day."

"And del Norte will be leaving after that?"

"I'm sure he will. He never stays long."

He swatted at an early deerfly, his expression taut, as if he wanted to say something but couldn't quite find the words.

Finally Easton sighed.

"What's on your mind, Trace?"

"I know it's none of my business but I'm worried about you."

"You don't need to worry about me," she lied. "I'm fine."

He reached for her gloved hand even though it was quite obviously covered in dirt. "I don't like that he's here."

His hand was big and warm and somehow comforting, but she still forced herself to slip her hand free, using the excuse of taking of her gloves and shoving them in her back pocket.

"I can't kick him out. This is his home as much as it's mine, Trace."

"Maybe technically. But everyone knows this is really your place. You're the one who has run things singlehandedly for the last few years. You're the one who stuck it out while everybody else took off. What is Cisco, really, but some vagabond petty criminal out for the next thrill?"

She had said nearly those same words to him earlier, but now she had to dig her nails into her palms to keep from defending him.

"Cisco would never hurt me, Trace. We practically grew up together."

He reached out suddenly as if to caress her cheek, but instead he pulled a stray leaf out of her hair.

"I'm sure you think you know the man. I understand that and can respect it. But something's off with him."

She frowned. "What do you mean?"

"I've spent the last twenty-four hours checking the usual sources to see if I can find out a little more about him and what he's been doing the last few years."

She stared. "You ran a background check on him?"

"I made a few calls. Looked up a few things. He's in my town, East. He shows up out of the blue with a baby that's supposedly not his. I need to know if he's going to bring trouble with him."

Oh, Cisco had already done that. She closed her eyes briefly, her mind on that midnight kiss. When she opened them, she found Trace Bowman watching her out of concerned green eyes.

"What did you find out?" she asked.

"Very little, which bothers me just as much as if he had a lengthy rap sheet. The man's a ghost, Easton. He has left very little trail, something highly suspicious."

He hesitated for a moment, then reached for her hand again. "Whatever he's up to down south, I have serious doubts it's anything legit."

Hearing the words she had long suspected from an officer of the law was a stark slap of reality.

"You don't have evidence he's done anything wrong, though."

"No. He's covered his tracks. Or someone else has

done it for him. That doesn't make me any more comfortable having him here."

Was Cisco lying about Belle? Was the baby somehow part of some nefarious scheme? No, she couldn't wrap her head around it. He would never put a baby in harm's way. Or her. Somehow she knew that with equal conviction.

"I don't know him anymore, Trace. I'll freely admit that. But I do know he won't hurt me. The baby's aunt is coming later today for her and then Cisco will return to whatever he's up to and I can get back to running my ranch."

"Until he comes back and disrupts everything again."

Her head and her heart ached to think of years spent waiting for his next appearance. "Right."

"It's probably only a matter of time until the next bar fight kills him."

"Don't say that," she whispered. "Oh, please, don't say that."

He gave her a long, careful look and for a moment the only sound in the garden were the bees buzzing around Jo's perennials and the wind soughing through the trees.

Finally he sighed. "It's him, isn't it?"

She didn't pretend to misunderstand what he meant.

"I don't want it to be," she whispered miserably, sinking onto Jo's favorite bench.

He joined her and stretched out his legs. "You can't force feelings that aren't there."

To her vast relief, his expression seemed more rueful than genuinely hurt.

"I care about you, Easton," he went on. "I think with a little effort on both our parts, that could grow into more than just a pretty good friendship."

"I want that, too."

"Part of you might. But I'm guessing a big part of you is still tangled up with him. Maybe it always will be."

Oh, she hoped not. She was tired of being miserable and lonely.

She wanted to ask Trace to give her more time before he completely gave up on her, but she recognized how unfair that would be. Not many men would be willing to wait around for a woman to fall out of love with someone else.

"I'm sorry," she murmured.

She felt his shrug where their shoulders touched and his smile was tinged with regret. "Same here. But I'm sure we'll both somehow survive."

They sat for several moments in silence and she watched the bees move from flower to flower, always leaving something behind while they took what they needed.

"I've been in love with Cisco since the day he showed up at the ranch," she finally said. "He was twelve. I was nine. That day, as he stood there in jeans that were about three inches too short and raggedy, holey tennis shoes, I just knew. I...keep trying to break free, but every time I think I can, he comes back for a few days or maybe a week and I'm right back there, tangled up in knots."

"Does he know?"

She let out a breath. She hadn't even voiced the words to her closest friends. Even if they might suspect, they didn't *know*. Yet here she was spilling all her foolish, ridiculous hopes and dreams to the man she had hoped might help her finally get over them.

"No one does."

One of Suzy's puppies wandered over to them and licked at Trace's boot. He scooped it into his lap and scratched its ears. At the gesture, Easton suddenly, absurdly, felt the sting of tears.

He was the sort of man she wanted to love. Good and decent, committed to his family and keeping his town safe. They could have a good life together, if she could only get Cisco del Norte out of her system.

Suzy apparently felt her puppy had been out of her care long enough. She wandered over to them and waited patiently at Easton's side until Trace set the pup back down in the dirt.

"There you go, Mama. See, safe and sound."

She didn't doubt he would take care of a woman with that same tender care.

"I don't want to see you hurt, Easton."

She already had been. She thought about the pain she had already endured, those months of deep loneliness and fear and then the ache of her empty arms. But she had endured. She had learned she was stronger than she ever imagined she could be.

"I appreciate that, Trace."

"Maybe you should use his time here to throw your cards out onto the table. Tell him how you feel. See if he might feel the same. Maybe that's what's always been keeping you from getting over him and moving on somewhere else, because some part of you is still hanging on to some kind of hope for the two of you."

She opened her mouth to protest, then closed it again. He was exactly right, she suddenly realized.

Cisco had turned to her after Guff died. He had held her with breathtaking tenderness. The kiss they had shared only the night before was evidence that heat still sizzled between them and she knew it wasn't only one-sided.

Was it possible one tiny corner of her heart was ridiculous enough to hang on to the vain hope that Cisco would admit he loved her? That he would come to see he couldn't possibly leave her again?

"I...you could be right," she said.

"Listen to me, giving you advice on how to get together with another guy, one I don't trust and don't particularly like. I've got to be crazy, right?"

"I think you're wonderful," she said.

He gave a laugh that was half groan. "Too bad you don't mean that the way I'd like you to."

"Seriously, Trace. I...this isn't going to come out right, but you're the first man who's made me want to stop being so hung up on...well, the impossible."

His laugh was rueful and utterly charming. "I guess that's something."

She leaned her head sideways against his shoulder for a moment, deeply grateful for his friendship.

"If anything changes after this visit of del Norte's, you know where to find me," he said after a moment. "Even if you just need an ear. I'm not exactly an expert at girl talk, but a good cop learns early how to listen."

"Thanks, Trace. I mean it."

Something subtly changed in the atmosphere, like ripples of energy from a faraway explosion. She glanced toward the back porch suddenly and there he was. Cisco stood watching them, his expression shuttered. He didn't have the baby in his arms, so Easton assumed Belle was sleeping.

Trace followed her gaze and she felt his muscles tense.

"I say we give him something to chew on," Trace murmured. A dimple flashed in his cheek.

Before she could ask what he meant, he dipped his mouth to hers, angling his neck so that all Cisco could see was the back of his head while he delivered what Easton could only guess was a very accurate impression of a passionate embrace, when in reality their mouths were barely touching.

By the time he pulled away, Easton didn't know whether to laugh or smack him. Her cheeks felt as if she'd just spent all day in the sun.

"You can thank me later." He winked at her and stood up. "Walk me to my truck?"

She complied, careful not to look toward the house to see if Cisco was still watching them.

"Be careful, okay?" Trace said after he opened his vehicle door.

"I will. Thank you."

He gave that rueful smile again, climbed into his vehicle and headed back down the driveway.

She watched after him for a moment, turned to return to the garden, then gave a gasp when she found Cisco standing only a few yards away from her. How in the world did a big man like him manage to move so soundlessly? The image of that mountain lion loomed in her head again and she shivered.

With his shaggy too-long hair, that hint of razor stubble and his faded jeans and snug T-shirt that showed off the tattoo on his forearm, he looked wild and dangerous.

"So you and the cop, huh? Looks serious."

How was she supposed to answer that? Considering that Trace had only kissed her to make Cisco jealous, she couldn't very well agree. She said nothing, which Cisco apparently interpreted as assent.

"That's good. From what I hear, he's a good man."

His casual words slid like ice shards into her throat. A good man. He couldn't make it any more obvious that he wanted nothing more than to push her toward Trace. He almost sounded relieved, damn him.

She reached down to pick up the trowel. "That's funny," she said, unable to keep the bitterness from her voice. "He was just saying the opposite about you."

A muscle tightened in his jaw and something bleak flashed in his eyes. "You should listen to him," he said, then turned abruptly and headed back inside the house, the back porch door banging shut behind him.

She drew in a deep breath, then another, then another, Trace's words echoing in her ears.

Maybe that's what's always been keeping you from getting over him and moving on somewhere else, because some part of you is still hanging on to some kind of hope for the two of you.

Trace was right. She had to know.

Now she only had to find the courage to ask him.

Cisco gripped the top rail of one of the kitchen chairs so tightly that he could feel the slats digging into his palms.

He squeezed his eyes shut, trying to block out the image of her in Bowman's arms. His chest felt like it was on fire and he had an insane urge to overturn every single chair in the kitchen, break all the china, grab the entire kitchen cabinets off the wall and hurl them to the floor.

He took a deep breath, working fiercely to calm himself. He had no right to be jealous. He wanted Easton to be happy. He hated thinking about her living here alone with no one to laugh with or share her life.

She had suffered great loss and pain, first her parents and then her aunt and uncle who had been surrogate parents. She deserved a good man like Bowman, someone free to take care of her, to look out for her, to make her smile.

She lived alone here at the ranch, throwing everything she had into it. He figured it was time she took a little joy for herself.

Trace Bowman appeared to besotted. He was the sort of man who would cherish a woman like Easton. He wouldn't try to stamp out her independence, the strong, courageous traits she had learned from Jo and Janet, her own mother.

If the Pine Gulch police chief could give Easton all the things in life she deserved, Cisco needed to just get the hell out of the way and let him.

He looked around the kitchen, familiar and comforting. The silly little clock above the stove Guff had brought back for Jo from a stock trip to Denver. The battered iridescent plastic tumblers he remembered winning at the county fair one year when he was maybe fifteen that Jo had insisted on displaying as proudly as if they were bone china. The kitchen table, where he and the others had learned to laugh and share and become a family.

Whether she ended up with Bowman or somebody else, Cisco wouldn't come back here after she married. How could he? The idea of seeing her settled, in love, round and glowing with another man's child, would rip him apart.

So he would just head back down south and stay there this time. When he finally washed out and outlived his usefulness to the various agencies who used his skills, he would just buy a shack on some beach in Mexico and spend the rest of his life in flipflops and cutoffs, casting a line out for his dinner and trying to forget Cold Creek Canyon and home and Easton.

A half hour later, he had locked most of his lousy mood away and was making a sandwich with leftover roast he found in the refrigerator when Easton walked into the kitchen from outside.

He didn't know how to interpret her expression, which seemed upset and wary at the same time.

She crossed to the sink and turned on the water to wash her hands. "If Aunt Jo could see how I've let her garden go the last few years, I'm afraid she would have a few choice words for me."

"You've had your hands full with everything else. I'm sure Jo would understand you're trying your best."

She flashed him a quick look. "You think so?"

"You know how Jo was. Always after the silver lining. Selective myopia, I think. She wanted to see only the best in everyone."

"True enough."

"Just look at Quinn, Brant and me. She took three rough, difficult boys who were probably headed for mis-

erable lives and turned us all into pretty decent men."
He paused. "Well, most of us, anyway."

She frowned. "Stop it."

He should just shut up right now, but the words seem
to ooze out of him like filthy sludge. "Quinn runs one of
the biggest shipping companies in the Northwest. Brant
is a highly decorated officer in the Army Rangers. And
I spend my days drinking tequila and working on my
tan, right? Jo and Guff must be so proud."

She shut off the water with jerky movements. "Oh,
cry me a river, Cisco. If you don't like your life, do
something about it. Come back to the States. Call Quinn
for a job."

"My life is fine," he lied. "Maybe what I don't like
is everybody's judgmental attitude. You all wonder why
I don't come back to visit more. Maybe because I'm so
tired of you all looking down on me when you don't
know one damn thing about me anymore."

Okay, maybe he hadn't quite worked out all of his
bad mood. Her eyes widened at the outburst, but before
she could answer, his cell phone rang.

He wanted to ignore it, but a quick check of the
caller ID had him scrambling for it. "Yeah. Hello," he
growled.

A crackle of static and then silence met him on the
other end and then a hesitant voice spoke. "Um, hello.
This is Sharon Weaver."

He could hear crying children in the background and
what sounded like a considerable degree of chaos.

"Hi, Sharon," he greeted John's sister. "Is everything
okay?"

"Not really. My van is having some trouble. The
cooling system or something like that. I don't know.

It's in the shop and we're waiting for a part. So I'm still staying with my mom in Helena and I'm afraid I won't be able to make it to Pine Gulch to pick up Belle until later than I expected tomorrow."

One more day. He wasn't sure how he felt about that. Spending another day with Belle would be a delight. He wouldn't have expected it but she had wrapped her firm little fists tightly around his heart.

More time with Belle was no hardship. Staying even another hour in the same house with East, on the other hand, was quite a different matter.

"No problem. Tomorrow should be fine. I'll watch for you."

"Janie, chase after your brother, would you?" Cisco had to hold his phone a little away from his ear as she raised her voice to be heard over whatever craziness was going on at her end. "Austin, get that out of your mouth. Right now, before you puke."

She finally turned back to their conversation. "Sorry about that. They're a little tired of being cooped up in my parents' tiny house."

"Are you sure you've got room for one more?"

She paused just a moment, but it was enough to send ice cubes rattling around in his gut. "We'll have to, won't we?"

If he hadn't been trained to pick up on every subtle clue people might drop in conversation, he might have missed the slight hesitancy in her voice.

Was she having second thoughts about taking the baby? He certainly hoped not. What the hell was he supposed to do if she changed her mind?

He wasn't going to give her a chance to do it over the

phone. "We'll watch for you tomorrow, then. Thanks for letting me know. See you later."

He wrapped up the call as quickly as halfway decent manners allowed, before she could back out.

"Everything okay?" Easton asked after he hung up.

He set the phone down on the table. "I hope so. Sharon Weaver sounds like a woman being pulled in too many directions."

"Taking on a child when you already have several of your own is bound to make any sane woman a little nervous."

He frowned at his closed cell phone, unable to shake his lingering unease at Sharon's hesitant reaction. "Right. And her father just died, only a few months after her brother's death. It has to be a lot to absorb all at once."

Easton nodded, sympathy for a woman she didn't even known turning her eyes an even darker blue.

"Looks like we're stuck in Pine Gulch another day." He paused. "You know, I'm sure Brant and Mimi wouldn't care if I took Belle up to Western Sky until she gets here tomorrow."

Her hands stopped slicing a tomato for her own sandwich and she stared at him. "Why would you want to do that?"

He could come up with a dozen reasons. The little dimple in her cheek he couldn't stop staring at. That luscious waterfall of blond hair he wanted surrounding him. The cinnamon taste of her mouth and the heady little sounds she made when he kissed her.

The man who had just been kissing her in the garden.

That was enough to start.

"You're obviously busy and we're in the way," he answered.

"Oh, cut it out." She set down the knife with a clatter. "You and Belle can stay here as long as you need. I've told you that."

"Even though you would rather we were on the other side of the county right now? And I imagine Chief Bowman would prefer me to stay in a different hemisphere."

"Trace is worried about me. That's all."

Cisco raised an eyebrow. "What does he think will happen?"

"Probably what already has," she murmured.

They gazed at each other for one long, charged moment and his mind flashed to the night before—of her soft, sweet response, of her curves pressing against him, of the heat churning through him like a forest fire flareup and the erotic sound of his name of her lips.

Before he could figure out how to answer, they both heard a plaintive cry over the intercom.

"Saved by the Belle," he muttered.

"Very funny." She made a face that reminded him forcefully of her mischievous younger self and how he used to adore making her laugh.

He started to rise but Easton shook her head. "Stay here. I'll get her."

He slid back into his seat and watched her go, wondering how he was going to keep his hands off her for one more day.

Chapter Seven

She was desperately grateful for any excuse to escape the simmering tension. Easton pressed a hand to her twirling stomach as she headed up the half-log stairs toward the fretting baby.

Whatever appetite she might have worked up out in Jo's garden had completely fled now. Drat the man. Why couldn't they manage to spend five minutes together without all the subcurrents seething between them like the spring runoff running high and fast down Cold Creek?

With a fierce pang, she missed the days when he used to tease her and laugh with her. Of all the boys, Cisco had been the most fun, always ready with a story or a joke or some funny observation that would crack them all up.

She hurried into the nursery and found Isabella sitting up, rubbing her eyes that swam with tears.

"Hey, there, sweet girl," she murmured to the baby.

Belle's dark curls were flattened on one side and her nose had dripped along with her tears, but she was still a beautiful child. When she saw Easton, the baby gave that wide, wholehearted grin of hers and Easton felt another fissure crack through the hard shell she thought she had formed around her heart.

Another one threatened to break apart when Belle held her chubby little arms out eagerly for Easton to pick her up.

She obediently lifted her from the crib and pressed her cheek to Belle's silky-soft curls. Was there anything in the world more sweetly adorable than a warm, cuddly baby just waking up from a nap?

Too warm, she realized with sudden chagrin.

"Oh, dear," she said after she had checked out the situation. "You're soaked through, pumpkin. Let's get you out of those wet things."

Belle giggled and reached for Easton's tiny silver hoop earring in response.

Easton laid her on the changing table and preemptively handed her a squeaky toy mouse so she wouldn't squirm too much.

When she saw the somewhat lopsided diaper, something soft and tender fluttered in her heart. Cisco wasn't the world's best diaperer, but it touched her to see his inexpert attempts, especially when she considered that he had to deal with his own injuries.

She pulled the diaper up and fastened the sides and then changed her into a darling little pair of jeans and a red polka dot long-sleeved shirt she pulled from the open suitcase by the changing table.

She tousled the curls out a little with her fingers.

"There. Now you're not lopsided," she said and Belle giggled again.

She had to admit, she probably wasn't much better than Cisco at the whole diapering thing. Oh, she had no problem dealing with orphaned calves, but her practical experience with human babies was limited to the precious few opportunities she had enjoyed with her honorary niece and nephew.

Since she wasn't in a rush to relinquish Belle to Cisco's care—or to face him again just yet—she spread one of the baby blankets on the floor and scattered a few toys for the baby, then set her down in the middle of them.

Belle immediately went for her favorite stuffed dog and shoved a floppy ear into her mouth.

"You love that thing, don't you?" Easton smiled and was rewarded with that adorable wide grin. "I should take you out to see the real thing. My doggy Suzy has five chubby little puppies. I think you'd love them."

Belle slithered commando-style toward her and presented the drooly dog to her, much like one of the barn cats offering her the prized gift of a dead mouse.

"You keep it," Easton said, though she felt another barrier crumble.

Belle rolled to her back and played for another moment or two, but then she was back, her arms out for Easton to pick her up. Had she always been this cuddly or was it a reaction to her confusion over losing her mother?

Whatever the reason, something warm and sweet trickled through Easton's heart as she complied. "You are a darling, aren't you?" she said with a smile. "I hope your aunt loves you as much as I—"

She jerked her mind away from that dangerous thought. She couldn't let herself love Belle. Oh, she could care about the little girl. A person would have to be a hard-hearted monster not to think Belle was sweet and adorable.

But she was leaving soon.

Just like everyone always left.

Easton pushed away the self-pity. Jo would have chided her for focusing on the negative instead of simply enjoying the small, peaceful moments while she could.

She rested her cheek against Belle's soft curls and closed her eyes, determined to do just that, to concentrate on the not inconsiderable delight of a small, warm weight on her lap and the intoxicating scent of powder and baby shampoo.

She sensed Cisco's presence before she actually heard any sign of him. When she opened her eyes, she found him standing in the doorway watching her and Belle, a strange, intense light in his eyes that disappeared as soon as their gazes met.

He was the first to speak. "Everything okay? I was wondering what was taking you two so long."

"Sorry. She was wet clear through, so I had to change her clothes and then we decided to play for a moment."

"I guess you figured out I'm not the greatest at changing diapers."

She smiled a little, grateful they could communicate on fairly neutral grounds about this at least. "I was just thinking what a good job you have been doing taking care of her," she answered.

"For a bumbling idiot, anyway."

"I'm completely out of my comfort zone with her, too, Cisco."

"You're wonderful with her," he protested. "Much more comfortable than I am."

"Listen to us, talking about who is more inept with babies."

He laughed, a low, husky sound, and she instantly wished for a return to the tense awkwardness between them. She almost thought she would prefer that to this subtle, soft warmth seeping through her.

"You really are wonderful with her," he answered. "I think you need one of your own. So why haven't you already married somebody like Bowman and filled the house with little rug rats?"

Careful what you wish for, she thought as his words sliced through her and all the tension rushed back.

You need one of your own.

Her arms tightened around Belle while she caught her breath. She couldn't look at him, not at all sure how to answer. She certainly couldn't tell him the truth.

"I guess it just hasn't happened for me yet. But then, running Winder Ranch doesn't leave me much time to socialize."

"Well, someday you're going to be a wonderful mother."

She somehow managed to summon a smile and had to hope he couldn't read the pain she was quite sure she couldn't completely hide.

"I was just telling Belle about Suzy's puppies. Why don't you rest for a while? Belle and I can give you a break while we go out to see the pups."

"Yeah, I'm not a real big fan of naps."

"But you're not usually recovering from an infected stab wound, right?"

"Depends on the time of year."

Her mouth tightened. She was almost positive he meant the words as a joke, but she couldn't find any humor in his casual acceptance of his hazardous life and his unwillingness to change it.

"It's a lovely afternoon out there. Maybe I'll just come out to see the puppies with you," Cisco said. "Do you think Suzy will mind?"

"I'm sure you'll charm her, just like you do with every other female."

"You being the exception to the rule," he murmured.

Ha. She all but *defined* the rule. From the time she was nine years old, she had been helpless to resist him and she was fairly certain he knew it.

Maybe you should use his time here to throw your cards out onto the table. Tell him how you feel. See if he might feel the same. Maybe that's what's always been keeping you from getting over him and moving on somewhere else, because some part of you is still hanging on to some kind of hope for the two of you.

Trace's words echoed in her mind. This afternoon might be the perfect time to talk to him, if she could only gather her nerve.

An hour later, Easton watched Cisco on the straw-strewn concrete floor of the barn, Belle in his lap and puppies crawling over both of them.

For the first time in years, he seemed to have dropped that cynical mask. He seemed younger, somehow, easier.

Every moment with him like this, soft and relaxed and smiling, gouged at her heart with sharp, wicked talons.

He was making her fall in love with him all over again. How ridiculous of her to suppose she had any chance of opening her life and her heart to someone else when she was still so tangled up with him and was so afraid she always would be.

The future without him stretched ahead, bleak and depressing. She was angry, suddenly, at herself and at him.

"Having puppies crawling all over you can't be very hygienic when you're trying to recover from an infected stab wound, wouldn't you agree?"

"I'm sure it's fine."

"How am I supposed to trust the judgment of someone who gets into bar fights in the first place?"

To her mixed relief and disappointment, the shutters clanged shut over his expression again. "Don't fuss, East. I'm fine."

"Forgive me if I have doubts. Thirty-six hours ago you were so delirious you didn't know where you were."

"And now I do," he retorted.

She opened her mouth to press on, then closed it again. What was she doing here? Picking a fight, to what end?

If all she had with him were these rare, priceless moments, how foolish to waste them with silly bickering. Whatever happened with Isabella, he would be leaving soon.

That was exactly why she was fighting with him. She couldn't bear to think about him leaving again—but that didn't mean she had to be bitchy and small, to raise her hackles like one of the barn cats every time she felt threatened or afraid.

She scratched Suzy's ears and resolved to try harder to savor the moment instead of worry about the future. "Do you remember when Uncle Guff's old dog Gert had puppies? Her first litter?"

When he laughed like that, he lost all the hard, cynical edges. "Guff planned to breed her with some champion border collie from Wyoming, didn't he?"

"Right." She smiled at the memory. "Instead, she somehow hooked up with my mother's rascal of a chow, Dudley."

"Whenever I hear somebody say all puppies are adorable, I only have to remember the result of that particular genetic soup. I've got to say, that was the butt-ugliest litter of puppies that ever existed."

"In a completely darling way," she protested.

"If you say so." He smiled and shook his head as he reached to stop Belle from yanking one of the puppies' tails.

"She's a little handful, isn't she?"

"Doesn't surprise me a bit. Her dad never met a good time he didn't like."

He hadn't referred much to Belle's father before, only her mother, Easton realized. "Were you close friends with them?"

His expression turned guarded again. "You could say that. Friends and…business associates."

"What sort of business?"

She knew he wouldn't offer a straight answer even before she asked the question. He never did.

This time he studied her for a long moment and she thought he would tell her. He finally glanced away, but not before she thought she saw a bleak shadow in his eyes. "Oh, you know. A little of this, a little of that."

His familiar and completely expected evasiveness threatened to break her new resolve not to fight with him.

"Sure." Some of her bitterness trickled out. "What's a few stab wounds between friends?"

A muscle flexed in his jaw. "East—"

"Never mind." She forced a smile. "I don't want to fight with you today. Here, let me take her for a minute."

She lifted the baby from him and pulled one of the puppies with them. For a few moments, she enjoyed the sweetness of a giggling child and a wriggling puppy.

She thought Cisco was done with the subject of Belle's father and their so-called business dealings, but after a few moments, he spoke in a low voice.

"If circumstances were different, I would come back, East. Believe me, I would. But I can't. I have…obligations down there."

She cuddled Belle closer. Obligations. Had a nice sinister ring to it, as if he was indebted to some organized crime boss or drug cartel.

Or as if he had a wife and a passel of kids tucked away somewhere.

"You don't owe me explanations, Cisco. It's your life, as Jo so often reminded me."

He almost told her everything, right there in the Winder Ranch hay barn, amid the smell of hay and manure and puppies, with dust motes floating like shimmery gold flakes in the slanting afternoon sun.

He was so damn tired of the lies and the subterfuge. The urge to pull her close, to rest his chin on her head and confess all his sins and mistakes was overwhelming.

He curled his fingers into a fist. He couldn't. The idea of dragging her into the harsh ugliness of his world was as repugnant as chewing on one of those old worn leather bridles hanging on the wall.

He was lousy at protecting the women in his life, but he could at least keep Easton from knowing the gritty details.

Belle gave a sudden loud sneeze, probably from puppy dander or all the dust and hay. Whatever the cause, the sound startled her enough that she let out a squawking cry.

"Hush, sweetheart. You're okay." Easton tried to soothe her, but Belle had apparently decided she'd had enough of barns and puppies.

"Do you want to take her and I'll put the puppies back in the stall?"

"I've got them," he said.

By the time he had lifted four wriggly puppies and set them back inside their warm bed with Suzy, his stomach muscles ached and his head started to throb.

When he closed the stall door and returned, he found Belle tugging Easton's braid. She tried to put it in her mouth, but Easton grabbed it away before she could.

"Looks like somebody's getting hungry for dinner, aren't you, little bug?"

Belle beamed at him and Easton smiled at her. The sight of the two of them there in the middle of a sunbeam in the old barn curled into his chest. His throat felt thick, suddenly, with emotions he didn't want to face.

He would treasure the images of this afternoon and would take them with him when he returned, to join the other memories of Easton that sustained him when he was wading knee-deep in the muck and misery of his life.

Although he had tried his best to hide the ache of his injury, Easton must have sensed he still wasn't a hundred percent. She insisted on carrying Belle to the house and setting her into the high chair in the kitchen.

She even washed the little girl's hands and face with a soapy cloth, wary of dog germs, he imagined.

"I'd better take care of chores," Easton announced after she finished cleaning up and had sprinkled toasted oats cereal on the high chair tray for Belle to nibble. "Can you handle things in here for a while?"

"Why don't I do that for you?" he offered. "I think I can still remember which end of a horse to feed."

She raised a skeptical eyebrow and he wondered just how well she could read the signs that he still wasn't feeling his best.

"Thanks for the offer, but Burt and I have a system in the evenings. It would take longer for me to explain what to do than it would for me to just do it myself."

She sat on the bench by the back door while she switched to her muck boots and he wondered how many times she sat there by herself in this big, empty house.

"I should be back in an hour or so. Call my cell if you have any problems."

He nodded and he and the baby both watched her

leave. Belle made a little sound of distress after the outside door closed behind her.

"Yeah, sweetheart," he muttered. "I know just what you mean."

This was getting to be a rotten habit.

Easton woke just before midnight, her attention instantly focused on the intercom. Had that been Belle she heard? She tried to blink away the wispy tendrils of sleep, the half-forgotten dreams.

Her room was dark, illuminated only by the face of her alarm clock and a pale shaft of moonlight filtering through the curtains.

She didn't hear anything further and wondered if she had imagined things. On the other hand, maybe the intercom was somehow broken. After a moment of listening, Easton slipped from her bed. She hated the idea of Belle fretting alone in a strange bed. Checking wouldn't hurt a thing and would put her mind at rest so she could sleep again.

She pulled on her robe and found her slippers, then headed out into the darkened hallway.

In Belle's room, she found the baby sleeping soundly, no sign that she had even stirred in the last hour.

Easton shook her head at her own foolishness. She used to hear a baby cry often in her nightmares, seeking a mother who never came.

Belle's mother would never come again when she cried, but Easton had to pray her aunt would embrace the darling little girl and welcome her into her family.

A few more hours. She tried not to think about what would be coming in the morning. Better to focus on the lovely afternoon and evening she had spent with the baby and, yes, with Cisco.

After she had finished with chores, she had returned to the house to find Cisco had thrown together dinner for them, a delicious chicken pasta with ingredients he dug out of her neglected pantry.

Even though the air had remained charged between them, humming and popping with that subtle tension, she had opted to ignore it to focus instead on what she was certain were her last hours with them. They had ended up sitting out on Jo's porch swing to enjoy the sweetly scented May evening, the baby laughing between them with each movement.

Belle had been close to falling asleep from the steady rhythm—and Easton too, if she were honest, more relaxed than she'd been since Cisco showed up at the ranch.

He had been the one to announce he'd better give Belle a bath or they would all fall asleep on the swing and end up spending the night out there in the cold. Easton had insisted on giving Belle her bath, as much to protect Cisco from having to lean over the bathtub with his injuries as from her own desire to prolong her time with the little girl.

After Belle was bathed and changed, sleepy and warm in her arms, Easton had held her close for a long time on the rocking chair, until she feel asleep.

When she returned downstairs, she found Cisco still sitting on the porch swing, gazing out at the ranch in the pale, dusky light of sunset.

He looked…lost, somehow, and something twisted inside her.

"She get down okay?" he asked.

"Yes. She's been asleep for a while now, but I couldn't resist holding her for a moment. She's darling, isn't she?"

"Yeah."

She couldn't shake Trace's words of advice. *Tell him how you feel. See if he might feel the same.*

It would have been the perfect time for that sort of declaration. She could sit down beside him on the swing, grip the chain tightly in her fingers and spill out her feelings.

I've been in love with you since I was nine years old. You're everything to me. Please come home, Cisco.

She had dug her fingernails into her palms, turned to him and opened her mouth. "Cisco, I … "

But he had jumped up before the words were even out. "Think I'll hit the sack, too. I'm pretty tired from the antibiotics."

She hadn't known what to do, to say, except stare at him. "I…really?"

"Yeah. I'll see you in the morning."

She watched him hurry into the house, her nerves tangled and raw, wondering just why he was avoiding her.

Did he sense what she intended to say and hope to avoid any awkward lovesick confessions and the complications they would entail?

She sighed now, a tiny sound in Belle's dimly lit bedroom. Probably better that his abrupt exit had precluded her from saying anything. Better that she kept her big yap zipped, that she just accepted the harsh truth that anything real and lasting between her and Cisco del Norte was as unlikely as palm trees growing in the high pasture.

Belle stirred and rolled to her side, her little mouth suckling at air. Easton drew a breath into lungs that suddenly seemed lined with razor blades.

Oh, she would miss this little girl. After Belle and Cisco left, the ranch would seem deathly quiet.

How was it possible that one darling child could worm her way so easily into Easton's heart in such a short time, especially when she had been trying her best to guard against that very thing?

Something about this cheerful little baby tugged at her insides, made her want to gather her close and not let go.

But she had to let go. In a few hours, Belle's family would come for her and Easton would have to dig deep to find that elusive strength once again.

She reached a hand to Belle's soft curls but stopped a few inches shy of them, reluctant to wake her. She withdrew her hand and stood by the side of the crib for a moment longer, then finally turned to find her bed once more and froze.

Cisco stood in the doorway watching her and the baby. His hair was mussed from sleep, he wore only low-slung jeans unbuttoned at the top and his skin gleamed bronze in the glow from the Winnie the Pooh nightlight.

Nerves skittered through her, sharp and urgent. She wanted nothing more than to slink into the rocking chair and pull one of Belle's blankets over her head until he left.

Her emotions were too close to the surface right now for her to be cool and controlled around him.

Instead, she forced herself to move closer. He backed up into the hall and she followed him, tugging the door closed behind her.

"Has she been up?"

"I don't think so. I thought I heard her crying, but now I think I must have been imagining things. You didn't hear her cry out, did you?"

"No. Only you moving around in here."

He shifted just enough that she saw the outline of something hard and dark tucked into his waistband at the small of his back.

His gun. He couldn't even move around the ranch house without feeling the need to protect himself. It was a stark and rather sad discovery.

"I'm sorry I woke you," she said.

"You didn't. I was awake."

"But you were so tired earlier."

Something suspiciously like guilt flashed in his eyes, confirming her suspicion that he had pretended a need for sleep so he wouldn't be forced to be alone with her after Belle went to bed.

"I slept for a few hours. Sometimes that's all I need."

"Even when you're recovering from a knife wound?"

"Old habits and all that. Guess I'm still a night owl."

He gazed at her in silence for a moment and she was suddenly intensely aware of her nightgown, threadbare since even before Jo died eighteen months earlier. She could at least have picked a nightgown that didn't make her look like some dowdy maiden aunt.

"Um, so how are you feeling?" she finally asked.

"Still hurts like hell," he admitted, much to her surprise. "But at least the fever's gone and I'm no longer feeling like you've been dragging me behind Lucky Star for a few weeks."

"That's good."

Now. She should tell him now. The words hovered on her tongue, but in the end she chickened out. Not yet. She had one more day to get through with him. Once she told him how she felt, she couldn't take the words back and she was very much afraid of ruining even the little portion she had of him.

She couldn't think of anything else to say, even with all the thoughts zinging around in her head, so they stood in silence for a moment. The house was quiet around them, peaceful, and she could suddenly hear her heartbeat. She wanted desperately to step forward and kiss him again. The memory of the night before shimmered around them and she could almost taste him one more time.

She drew in a shaky breath and prayed he didn't notice. "Um, we should probably go to bed. I mean *back* to bed. Both of us. Separately."

Something dark flickered in his gaze and she thought she saw a pulse in his throat. "Right. That's probably a good idea."

"Good night, then." She escaped into her bedroom and closed the door, feeling like the world's biggest fool.

She could handle being an idiot, she thought as she climbed into her solitary bed. But she really hated feeling like a coward.

Chapter Eight

Easton's muscles hummed as she scooped another shovel full of sand into a bag. After two hours of this, she never wanted to see a shovel or a pile of sand again in her life.

"A couple more ought to take care of our second load." Burt closed the bag and hefted it into the pickup truck to join rows of others. "That should be enough for us to protect the hay up there."

She set down her shovel. "I hope so. We just need to hang on for a few more weeks, until the first hay cut of the season."

"Few weeks beyond that and we'll be moving the herd out of here and won't need it. Think we'll make it?"

"I don't know." She wiped at her forehead. "Why don't you call Dusty Harper and check if he has any hay to sell. This time of year, he might try to gouge us for it, but you can see if he'll give us a decent price."

"Will do. You okay down here while Mike and me take this last load up to the creek?"

"Should be."

Once more, she found herself deeply grateful for the endless workload of a cattle ranch that left her little time to brood about anything, especially not her own cowardice.

After she left Cisco standing in the hallway, she had tossed and turned for a long time before she finally fell asleep only a few hours before dawn. Of course she had dreamed again in the night. She should have expected it. In her dream, the two of them had been on Jo's porch swing enjoying a pleasant evening, but they couldn't seem to make the swing move in unison. His side had been swinging faster than hers and as a result, the whole thing moved crazily, chains jangling.

Suddenly a baby started to cry somewhere on the ranch. Easton jumped up and began to frantically search everywhere while the baby cried and cried and somewhere in the distance a mountain lion screamed.

She awoke when her alarm went off with her heart pounding, her pulse racing and her cheeks wet.

She hadn't wanted to spend the morning moping around the house, waiting for Belle's aunt and cousins to arrive, and she had been fiercely glad for the excuse to throw herself into sandbagging today after Burt called to tell her the creek was running higher than either of them had expected.

They should have moved the hay out when they had the chance, but a couple of pickup truck loads of sandbags would probably take care of the problem until the next crisis rolled along.

Once again, Winder Ranch had been her salvation

and once more she realized the healing power of hard work, throwing herself into mind-numbing physical labor to dull the edge of her emotional turmoil.

Move forward, Jo would have said. When you don't feel you can go another inch, just keep on riding until you get past the obstacles on the trail.

When Jo fell ill, Easton had been so grateful for the peace she found through work, for the steady comfort of routine. Ranch work had saved her again eighteen months ago when her aunt died, outlasting doctor's prognosis by a year.

She would get through this, too. Belle would settle in with her aunt. Cisco would return to his wandering ways. And Easton would throw herself back into the ranch. Who knows? With all the restless energy seething through her right now, she might be able to channel her efforts into making this Winder Ranch's most successful year.

"You listening at all to me, missy?"

She jerked her attention back to Burt, chagrinned at her rudeness. "Sorry. My mind was wandering."

"I reckon I know just what direction it was heading." He glowered toward the house. "Be good when some people leave, so the rest of us can get a little bit of work done around here again."

She set the shovel carefully aside and lifted the bag into the pickup truck. "I'm sure you'll have your wish in a few hours."

"I guess they'll be gone by the time we get back from setting these sandbags around the hay barn."

She had planned to help her crew with the work at the flood site and avoid the house for the rest of the morning, but as she stepped away from the bed of the pickup truck, she knew she couldn't do it. Coward she might be when it came to revealing her deepest emotions to Cisco, but she couldn't bear the idea of not saying goodbye to that darling baby for what might be the last time.

"You and the boys can handle this by yourself, can't you?"

He squinted at her. "I s'pose."

"I'd better stick close to the house, just in case."

Burt had known her since she was just a pig-tailed tomboy and he didn't look at all fooled.

"Be good when we can get some work done around here," he repeated gruffly.

She didn't bother to answer him, since she imagined she would be doing the work of two men in the foreseeable future, with all the emotions she would need to burn off in the coming days.

She waved him off and then headed back to the ranch house. Inside the back door, she kicked off her dusty, gritty boots, then followed the happy baby sounds to the great room, where she found Cisco on the floor watching Belle crawl around and explore.

His dark, glittery gaze lifted to hers and she was suddenly back in that darkened hallway the night before with heat simmering between them.

"Hey. You must have left the house early," he said.

She shrugged. "Our flooding situation has taken a turn for the worse, so I've been filling sandbags."

Belle, drawn by the sound of their voices, shifted her attention from a nubby ball that was a particular favorite of Joey's. Her features lit up when she saw Easton and she clapped her hands and squealed with delight.

The baby's reaction sliced at her heart with dagger

precision. She pictured another dark-haired baby, one she had only held for a moment before the doctors and nurses took him away and the hospital chaplain stepped forward with soft eyes and gentle hands.

She forced a smile, pushing the memories away. "Hey. there, sweetheart."

Apparently she wasn't as good as she'd hoped at masking her reaction.

"What's wrong?" Cisco asked quietly.

"What do you mean?" she stalled.

He frowned. "I don't know. Every once in a while, you get this look in your eyes. I don't know what it is, but you look...wrecked."

She drew in a shaky breath, hating that he could see her so clearly about some things and be so completely oblivious about others. "You're imagining things, Cisco. Everything's fine. Why wouldn't it be?"

He narrowed his gaze at her vehemence, which seemed wholly out of proportion to what he thought had been gentle probing.

He had seen those shadows in her eyes at random moments before and had always assumed it had something to do with him and his stupid mistakes with her. He knew she had to be angry with him for letting the situation between them get out of hand after Guff's death, for taking advantage of her and assuaging his hunger for her when they were both grief-stricken, vulnerable.

But just now he had seen something else in her eyes, an old, deep sadness and he didn't have the first idea how to make it right.

"Any word from Belle's aunt?" she asked.

"Yes, actually. She called a few moments ago. She's just outside town, trying to find Cold Creek Canyon Road. I gave her directions. I expect she'll be here any minute."

Panic flickered in blue eyes he always thought were the exact color of the sea off Cartagena.

"So soon? We'd better hurry to find all her things."

He gestured to Belle's bag, already loaded and ready to go. "They're here. I packed everything earlier this morning."

If he thought she might commend him for his foresight, he was quite wrong. Her mouth hardened and her eyes turned frosty.

"You can't wait to be free of anything that remotely smacks of obligation, can you? That's so typical."

The swift deadliness of the attack just about took his breath away. He opened his mouth with a sharp retort, but then he looked closer and saw bleak misery in her eyes.

He felt as if she had just shoved him into the icy waters of Windy Lake.

Madre de Dios. Could he have been so wrong? All these years, he thought the tension simmering between them had been her anger at him for making love to her, taking her virginity when he had no right to it, when she had only followed him that night to offer comfort.

But maybe it wasn't regret and anger but something else, something deeper.

He thought of how hard she had pushed him to come back to the ranch, the way she seemed so distressed whenever he talked about leaving again.

His pulse kicked up a notch and he stared at her. He hadn't slept well after their encounter in the night, his mind whirling as he rehashed every interaction between them since he had come back to the ranch.

He didn't know what to think. Was it possible she wanted him back not because they were friends but because her feelings ran deeper?

Feeling at a disadvantage on the floor, he rose to his feet. He could push her and see how she reacted. It was old spy trick. Give a contact what you think he expects to hear and gauge his reaction to help decipher his true feelings.

"Yeah, by this time tomorrow, I should be on the beach with a *señorita* on my lap and a bottle in my hand."

He expected anger. Instead, her eyes turned dark with pain.

"Easton…"

Whatever he might have intended to say was shoved out of his mind by a flash of silver outside the window. He shifted his gaze and saw a minivan pull to a stop in front of the house.

Easton's features froze. Whatever he thought he saw there was hidden quickly as she worked to regain control.

"Looks like she's here."

"Right."

They stood frozen, both of them looking at Isabella. Even after the doorbell rang through the suddenly still house, neither of them rushed to answer.

"I guess we should probably get that," Easton finally said when the bell rang a second time.

He suddenly wanted to tell her no, to grab Easton and Belle and whisk them out the back door and into the mountains, where he could hide them and keep them safe.

Keep them his.

The splash of reality was just as cold as always. He had obligations, as he had told Easton. He didn't have time or room in his life to take on a baby, no matter how adorable, no matter how tenaciously she seemed to be hanging on to his heartstrings with her chubby little fingers.

And Easton.

He didn't have room for her either—and even if he changed that somehow, if he walked away from The Game, he wouldn't deserve her.

"I'll get it," he said and walked to the front door.

When he opened it, the woman standing on the front porch was a plump, female version of John Moore, with his sandy blond hair and the same bright blue eyes her niece had inherited.

She was holding a toddler on one hip and looked to be about six months pregnant. Two older children, maybe four or five, stood behind her, peeking around at him with big eyes.

"Hi. I'm Sharon Weaver. Are you Cisco del Norte?"

"I am."

Belle must have followed him to the entry. She made a noise to be picked up and he complied, ignoring how the movement set his gut on fire from his injury.

"Sharon, this is Easton Springhill, the owner of Winder Ranch," he said. "And this is your niece."

The woman's wary expression softened as she looked at Belle. "Her eyes are Johnny's. And mine, too, I suppose. I thought so from the pictures Socorro was kind enough to e-mail me after Belle was born, but I wasn't certain."

Easton stepped forward. "Won't you all come in?

Sit down, please. Would the children like a cookie and some milk? I think I've got some Oreos in the kitchen."

That seemed to be the magic word. The older two looked as if Easton had offered them chocolate-covered gold bars.

"That would be lovely. Thank you very much." Sharon Weaver looked wearily relieved as the two older children followed Easton to the kitchen, leaving her with only the one in her arms.

"Were you a good friend of Socorro's?" she asked after Easton and the children were gone.

"She and John were both friends." It wasn't the most adequate of terms, but it was accurate anyway.

"I can't say I was surprised to get your phone call that she had been killed. She seemed to live in a pretty rough world. Sad but not surprised."

She died a hero, giving her life to avenge terrible wrongs and to try to save untold others. But because that information was classified and the efforts against *El Cuchillo's* cartel ongoing, he couldn't divulge it— even to Soqui and John's family—without endangering them.

"Please, won't you sit down?"

"I'm good for a minute. I've been driving all morning and it feels good to stand, to tell you the truth."

She had just come from her father's funeral, he remembered. He saw the shadow of grief in her exhaustion.

"I'm sorry for your loss."

She accepted his condolences with a tired nod. "It wasn't really a surprise. My dad has had congestive heart failure for the last five years. But it's still not easy.

My mom's having a hard time, what with losing Johnny just a year ago."

She finally set the toddler down and rubbed at her low back.

A thin line of mucus dripped from the boy's nose. He swiped at it with one dirty hand before his mother could whip a tissue from her pocket. The kid jerked his head to get away from the tissue attack but eventually submitted for a few moments, then made his escape and wandered toward the spot where Belle was once more playing with her favorite stuffed puppy dog.

Cisco didn't necessarily consider himself a fastidious man—that pretty much disappeared fast in the field— but he found himself heartily wishing for some hand sanitizer after the kid reached out and snatched the dog away with those same grimy fingers.

He waited to see if Belle was going to cry, but she only looked bewildered, then picked up a different toy, which the other kid also snatched away.

Cisco had to fight the urge to rush over and tell the little brat a thing or two about picking on creatures smaller than he was.

"How old is your little boy?" he asked instead.

"That one? That's Austin. He'll be two next month. He's a real handful." She curved a hand over her stomach. "This one is a boy, too."

"When are you due?"

"I still have three months to go. Wouldn't you know, I'm going to have to suffer through the third trimester in the worst heat of the summer. Don't know why we haven't figured out yet how to plan these things better."

She looked completely exhausted. He thought of the

two older children who had gone with Easton into the kitchen and then how much work Belle alone had been for him and unease slicked through him.

"You seem like you have your hands full," he finally said. "How will you handle three children under age two?"

She gave a heavy sigh. "I don't know. I'll figure something out, I guess. What choice do I have?"

He didn't have an alternative. The only one he could think of was, of course, completely impossible.

"My brother and his wife wanted me and Sam, my husband, to raise Isabella here in the U.S.," Sharon went on. "We agreed to take on the responsibility of being named her guardians, knowing that both Belle's parents were living...precarious lives. No, the timing isn't the greatest, but I guess that can't be helped."

It bothered Cisco that she hadn't gone to the baby or picked her up. Belle was her niece and would be living with her family. He would have liked to see a little spontaneous affection, but he supposed he couldn't have everything.

"I'll admit, I don't know much about babies, but Belle is a great kid," he said, feeling uncomfortably like a used car dealer trying for the hard sell. "Even though I can tell she misses her mama, she's been very good-natured and easygoing. She rarely cries at all, just when she's really tired or hungry."

"That's good. My second one was a real crier. I thought I'd go crazy until he grew out of it."

"And she's smart as can be," Cisco went on. "She's not quite nine months old and she's already trying to say *dada* and pull herself up to stand."

She smiled a little. "Don't know if that's always a

good thing. The sooner they walk, the better they are at getting into things. Austin, get that out of your mouth, honey. She was playing with it."

Cisco couldn't take any more of the toddler tormenting the baby. If the kid took one more toy away from her, he was going to have to step in and snatch it right back from the little toy thief.

Since he figured that probably wouldn't make a good impression on Johnny's sister, he opted instead to scoop Belle up into his arms, out of the line of fire.

Somewhat to Cisco's relief, the pregnant woman finally seemed to tire of standing. She eased her bulk to the edge of the couch. When she held out her hands for Belle, he didn't know what else to do but surrender her.

Belle blinked at her aunt for a long moment, her long eyelashes wide.

Sharon was the first to smile. "Hey, there, little girl. I'm your aunt. This is your cousin Austin. He's a bit of a tease, but I'm guessing you'll soon figure out how to give back as good as you get."

Belle gnawed on her fist and then blew a raspberry and the little boy giggled.

"Those eyes." Sharon's voice was soft and rather sad. "They're so much like Johnny's."

"Pretty close, from what I remember."

"My brother was a good kid." Sharon gave him a hard look, as if daring him to contradict her. "I don't care what kind of trouble he was messed up in down there. I always knew he would eventually straighten himself out and come home. And then he met Soqui and everything changed."

The culture of secrecy around undercover agents

had never seemed so unfair to him. Didn't she deserve to know her that her brother, like his wife, had been everything that was heroic and honorable?

"Your brother was a good man, ma'am," he finally said. "One of the best I've ever known."

Instead of taking his words as the comfort he intended, she looked vaguely contemptuous. It took him a moment to realize why. As far as Sharon Weaver was concerned, he was just some low-life expatriate thug who had probably contributed in some way to her brother's downfall.

His jaw hardened. Fair enough, he supposed. He hadn't been able to save Johnny…or Soqui either.

"How would you like a big sister and a couple of big brothers?" Sharon asked Belle, who pursed her mouth as if considering the question with deep gravitas.

"Are you certain your husband is on board with this?" Cisco had to ask.

If he hadn't been watching closely, he might have missed the hint of unease in her expression. "He's… not exactly thrilled about having another child in the house when I'm due in a few months. But he signed the guardianship papers, too, and Sam is a man who honors his commitments."

Cisco really wanted to be enthusiastic about Belle's new family. Sharon seemed nice, even if she was tired and would undoubtedly have her hands full in the coming months. But he couldn't shake his vague unease that he was handing something rare and precious over to people without the first idea of her value.

"You have all the paperwork?"

"The custody transfer is all signed and notarized.

I'll leave my contact numbers with you, in case you run into problems with the legalities."

"And all her things are packed?"

He indicated her car seat and the suitcase he had haphazardly stuffed clothes and toys into during those crazy few days in Bogotá after everything went to hell.

"It should all be here."

Sharon released a heavy breath. "I guess that's it, then."

She studied Belle without any trace of joy or excitement at gaining a beautiful dark-haired daughter, only that same weary resignation.

Cisco's chest felt tight and his vague misgivings turned solid and real. He didn't want to do this. But what other choice did he have?

"She eats just about anything mashed up. Her favorite foods seem to be carrots and applesauce. She still has a bottle at night and at nap time. There's a couple cans of the kind of formula mix she's used to in there."

His stab wound was hurting like a son of a bitch, something he didn't think was a coincidence.

"Great. Thanks. I'll call you if I have any other questions."

"She's due for a nap, so she might sleep a good portion of the way to Boise."

She lumbered out of the chair and he tried to picture her trying to juggle a rambunctious toddler, a newborn and a sweet-natured Belle, along with a couple of older kids. A mother's attention could spread only so far. Which of those would suffer the lack of it? He could guess only too well.

"I'd like to be back home in Boise by dinnertime, so I'd best gather everyone up and be on my way."

He didn't know how to stop her, so he reluctantly waited while she grabbed her little boy by the hand, then followed her into the kitchen.

Easton and the older two children sat around the table rolling out Play-Doh she must have unearthed from somewhere.

Easton looked first at Belle in the other woman's arms and then at him and the emotion drenching her eyes broke his heart all over again.

"Look, Mommy." Obviously oblivious to the simmering tension, the little girl beamed at Sharon. "I made a snake."

Belle's aunt smiled at her daughter, although it seemed edged with impatience. "Can you tell the nice lady thank you and then we need to clean up our mess so we can get back home. Don't you miss your daddy? I know I do."

He had to admit, he was rather impressed when the children didn't whine or protest, simply began gathering up the cookie cutters strewn across the table.

She seemed like a nice woman and would probably be a loving mother to Belle, but he still couldn't seem to shake these blasted misgivings.

When the mess was cleaned to their mother's satisfaction, the children raced out the front door to their minivan.

"Here, let me hook her into her car seat and carry her out for you," he said to Sharon.

"Thanks," she answered.

He took the baby and had to swallow three or four

times when she patted his cheeks with those chubby little hands and gave him that adorable gummy grin.

He gave her a hug and kissed her cheek.

"You be a good girl, won't you?"

She smiled at him and his throat suddenly ached in a way it hadn't in years and he had to concentrate hard to focus on sliding her correctly into her car seat and buckling the straps.

She was probably too big to still be in this kind of carrier seat. That's what the lady at the rental place had told him, anyway, but he would just have to let her new family address that particular issue.

As he picked her up and headed out to the waiting minivan, Easton followed him with Belle's suitcase and she seemed determined to avoid his gaze.

When they reached the vehicle, he looked inside and winced at the three booster seats already taking up most of the available seats.

Add another car seat for Belle and one for Sharon's new baby and the poor woman wouldn't have an inch of room to spare.

He could only hope she and her husband would find room in their hearts for a big-eyed little girl with dark curls and an adorable smile.

Chapter Nine

She couldn't go through this.

Not again.

Panic clawed at Easton's chest and she needed every ounce of self-control to beat it back, to keep it from completely devouring her.

In a few moments, this sweet little baby was going to leave her life completely and the brutal pain of it clutched at her insides with icy fists.

She had lost one baby. Those dark days and the raw pain of it had faded over the years to a steady ache.

In the last few days she had fallen hard for Isabella, despite her best efforts to keep her emotions in check. Her pudgy little fingers and the determined way she chewed her stuffed dog's ears and the intoxicating scent of her soft, silky skin.

In a moment, this sweet little girl was going to be gone, purged from her life as if she'd never been.

Again.

She swallowed hard, panic fluttering just on the edge of her awareness.

A few more moments. She could make it through a few more moments and then she would fall apart.

Cisco carried the car seat out to the minivan, while Belle's aunt shepherded her other children into their respective seats in the car.

She wanted to rush inside and curl up in fetal position on her bed and weep her heart out, but she forced herself to step forward once Belle was settled in her seat. Her chest aching, Easton kissed the little girl's cheek and closed her eyes as she felt Belle's cheek muscles move into a smile against her mouth.

"God bless, little bug."

The baby at last seemed to sense that something significant was going on. Her smile slid away and her little chin puckered. She reached her plump hands out to Easton, just another twist of the knife.

"I can't take you right now, sweetheart. I'm sorry." She stepped away as Belle started to rev up for a full-fledged wail.

"Don't forget, you have my cell number and the other contact number in the paperwork," Cisco said to her aunt over the baby's cries. "If you have any questions about her care or about the legal details, leave me a message and I'll return your call as soon as possible."

He sounded so matter-of-fact that Easton thought he must be the most callous person alive. She wanted to kick him. To scream and hit and throw something. To wail along with Belle until nobody could hear anything else.

"How long will you be here?" Sharon asked.

Cisco's gaze slanted briefly to Easton, then back to the other woman. "Not long. I don't know, exactly. I have…business back in South America."

Easton clenched her hands into fists. She was dying inside. She had to get out of here before she broke down.

Belle was full-fledged wailing now, her cries filling the air. A muscle jumped in Cisco's jaw but he did nothing to comfort her. Instead, he stepped away and her aunt leaned into the open door of the minivan.

"Hush now, little one. You'll be all right."

She seemed like a kind woman, down-to-earth and comfortable. Easton supposed she had to find solace in that.

"Holly, can you give your cousin a toy?" Sharon asked before turning back to Cisco and Easton with an apologetic look. "We'll be okay. I'm sure she'll fall asleep as soon as we get going."

"Car rides do tend to knock her out," Cisco offered.

Sharon closed the sliding minivan door and the three adults stood for a moment in an awkward tableau.

"We'd best get on the road, then. See if we can calm her down a bit," the aunt finally said. "I'll call you if I have any problems."

"Good luck," Cisco said.

He moved around the side of the vehicle and held the driver's door open for her. She climbed inside and started the van, then put the vehicle in gear and pulled away down the driveway with one last wave out the window.

And that was that.

Easton stood watching the van head down the long, winding lane for perhaps thirty seconds, fighting for control, pushing back images of the nurses taking a still, quiet, blanket-wrapped form out of her arms and the gaping pain they left in its place.

She couldn't stay here. Not with Cisco. She had to escape before it occurred to him to ask why saying goodbye to Belle, a baby she had known for only a few days, was affecting her so strongly.

"I've got to go check on the flooding situation up near the lake."

"Easton—"

She didn't wait for him to finish the thought, she only rushed away to the barn and saddled Lucky Star in record time. She was just shoving her boot into the stirrup to mount when he showed up in the doorway.

"You okay?"

"Just great. Get out of my way."

Her voice hardly even wobbled on the words, she was relieved to note as she pulled herself up and settled into the saddle.

"Want to talk about it?"

She walked the horse toward where he stood in front of the barn door. "No. I want you to get the hell out of my way or I'll let Lucky mow you down."

With a surprised look, he stepped aside just as she dug her heels into Lucky's side and spurred the horse to a gallop, whistling for Jack to come along.

She knew where she needed to go and she could count on Lucky to get her there fast—and on the wind racing past to dry her tears.

What was that about?

Cisco watched Easton tear up the trail on her big, sturdy gray, her border collie fast on their heels. He followed the trio's progress, concern warring with confusion. Even after Jo's death, he hadn't seen such anguish in her eyes. She looked completely shattered, as if something inside her had been crushed into a million pieces.

All this for a baby she hadn't even known existed four days ago? He didn't get it. Something was off. He had thought so ever since he arrived at the ranch with Belle. He thought of that sadness that sometimes flickered in her expression when she looked at the baby, the devastation he had seen earlier.

A moment later, she and her horse disappeared into the trees. He narrowed his gaze after them. Maybe she just needed a little time to settle down, to work out whatever had hit her so hard.

The sun pulsed down, warm for a late-May afternoon. He ought to go inside and pack his gear. Nothing to stop him from leaving now, when it would be least likely to result in an awkward scene.

He couldn't do it. Not when Easton was so upset. He couldn't bear knowing she was alone and in pain.

On impulse, he hurried into the house and quickly threw together a haphazard picnic lunch, though he had a feeling she wouldn't feel much like eating right now. He didn't either. But he knew from experience that sometimes a decent meal could at least make the world not seem quite so grim.

He stuffed sandwiches and some cut-up vegetables and fruit into a bag he could tie onto a saddle, added a couple of icy water bottles from the refrigerator, then grabbed a baseball cap off the hook by the door and headed out to the barn.

He hadn't ridden for a while. Opportunities to find

himself on horseback were few and far between in the dark world where he usually hung out. Probably the last time he'd ridden had been after Jo died and he took one of the horses deep into the backcountry for a couple of days of solitude, not trusting himself around Easton. He hadn't been at all sure he was strong enough to avoid a replay of what happened when Guff died, so he'd gone far enough into the wilderness where he figured no one could find him.

He picked Russ, his favorite, an easygoing but powerful bay gelding, and a short time later, the two of them were following the trail Easton had taken.

Cisco quickly fell back into the rhythm of the saddle. He had missed this. He would probably enjoy it much more if he wasn't so worried about her, but even so, few pleasures in his life compared to riding up a sundrenched trail with only the sounds of twittering birds, the jangle of tack, the rustle of the wind in the pines.

He followed the fork in the trail toward the upper pasture. Sandbags had been piled in a neat pyramid along the banks of the fast-moving creek and they seemed to be holding in the swift-flowing waters, from what he could tell.

No sign of Easton, though. He quickly scanned the area and saw no sign of life except for a couple of ground squirrels that bravely scampered along the new ridge created by all those sandbags.

He supposed he hadn't really expected to find her here. With a strong sense of inevitability, he wheeled Russ around and returned to the spot where the trail forked. Sure enough, now that he was looking for it, he saw clear evidence of horse's hooves in the mud leading in the other direction, farther up the narrow canyon.

He knew where she was going. It seemed unavoidable, inescapable.

Where else would it be? The trail led straight to Windy Lake and on the far bank of the lake was a small shelter he and his foster brothers built years ago for their frequent late-night fishing trips on the edge of Winder Ranch property.

When he was troubled or upset, he always escaped to the same place. When Guff died, this was where he had run.

And where she had found him.

The lake was only a mile or so from the house. When it came into view, long and silvery in the sunlight, the wild and restless beast that always seemed to prowl inside him sighed and settled.

He saw more evidence her horse had been this way, but he couldn't immediately see Easton or Lucky. He shaded his eyes with his hand and scanned the area for signs of life. He finally spotted the gray standing, reins dangling, in the tall grasses and spring wildflowers of the meadow near a thick stand of aspens.

His heart jumped. Her horse was there but where was Easton? Had she fallen? Was she hurt? In panic mode, he spurred Russ to a fast trot toward the other horse. He wouldn't survive if something happened to her. She had to be okay.

Jack raced toward them with two sharp barks, as if warning him to stay away, which only made him more concerned. Only when he and his mount reached the other horse's side did he finally see Easton.

Relief flooded through him like that spring runoff soaking the land.

She didn't appear to be hurt. She was perched in

a snow crook of one of the quaking aspens, a natural bench formed decades ago when the tree was young, when it must have been bent horizontal by heavy snows yet didn't break under the burden. He had always found it fascinating how those damaged trees maintained their crooked shape before zigzagging up to grow vertically once more.

She had been weeping. He could see the traces of it on her cheeks, in the redness of her eyes.

"Why did you follow me?" she said, her voice resigned. "I would think you, of all people, would be able to recognize when someone wants to be alone."

He scratched his cheek, acknowledging the truth of that. He had always been fiercely protective of those moments when he needed to escape the world. "Sorry, but I was worried about you. I didn't want you to be alone when you were so upset."

"I wasn't alone. I had Jack and Lucky."

"You know what I mean."

She picked at the bark of the aspen and didn't meet his gaze. "I spend most of my life alone, Cisco, now that Jo's gone. I'm pretty used to my own company."

He frowned. She should be married by now and filling the house with children of her own. She deserved a happily-ever-after, even if the thought of it seemed to shred his insides with jagged claws.

He was a selfish bastard. He wanted her to be happy, but he couldn't bear the thought of her being happy with someone else. This time he was the one who looked away and his gaze fell on a small bouquet of wildflowers she must have gathered—buttercups, trillium, camas, wild ginger. They rested at the base of another tree near the snow crook where she sat.

Higher up the pale aspen trunk, he had a vague impression of some sort of writing on the tree but he couldn't quite make out the words.

"What is this?" he asked, moving a little closer.

Something that looked suspiciously like panic flickered in her eyes and she slid down and moved in front of the trunk.

"Nothing. Just a tree," she said quickly. "There are still fly rods in the shelter if you want to use them."

As a diversionary tactic, it might have been a good one if not for his aching wound, which was currently making him question the wisdom of taking a horse on a winding mountain trail while he was still very much in recovery mode.

"Did you carve in the tree?" He tried to look around her. "Guff would have had your hide. You know how he used to lecture us about respecting the forest, about how carving initials in a trunk might last for generations but it can also introduce bacteria and can kill an otherwise healthy tree."

She said nothing, only continued to gaze at him with a look almost of defiance in her eyes.

"What is it?" he pressed her. "It looks like a memorial or something. Is it for Jo and Guff."

"Go away, Cisco. I don't want you here."

Her words hurt far worse than any thug's knife, though he knew they shouldn't. He wasn't part of her life. He had made sure of that. Could he blame her now if she preferred to push him away?

He almost acquiesced, almost climbed back on Russ and wheeled around back down the mountainside. But something pushed him to uncover her secrets. Somehow he sensed this tree was part of the mystery surrounding Easton, the sadness she couldn't always hide.

"Let me see."

"No."

"Come on, move."

For a long moment, she gazed at him, her eyes hollow and her features strangely motionless. Jack whined as if sensing the sudden tension. Then, just when Cisco was wondering if he wanted to push the matter enough to physically lift her out of the way, she finally stepped aside.

He took another step toward the tree and saw that she hadn't carved the words on a tree but on a small brass plaque mounted to the trunk.

Chance del Norte.

March 1, 2005.

My heart.

Everything inside him went still, a vast frozen wasteland.

"What is this?"

She said nothing, only reached down to scratch her dog's ears, not looking at him.

"Easton. Talk to me, damn it. Who is Chance del Norte?"

She looked extraordinarily beautiful, fragile and soft like a beam of sunlight, but when she lifted her gaze, her eyes were drenched with pain.

"Our son," she finally whispered.

His knees literally went weak, something he thought only happened in books and movies. He could feel the strength leave every muscle in his legs and he had to grip the rough, curling trunk of the aspen for support.

"Our...son?"

She nodded. "He had dark hair, lots of it, and a little dimple in his chin. I think he would have looked just like you."

"Our son."

How could it be possible? He thought of the one night they had spent together in the shelter beside Windy Lake, just a hundred yards away from here, when they had turned to each other in their shared grief over Guff's death.

He had used a condom. He remembered that much.

At least the first time...

He closed his eyes as he suddenly recalled turning to her in the night and the heat and passion that had flared between them again.

She had immediately fallen asleep in his arms, her muscles lax and each breath a tiny stir against his skin. But he hadn't been able to close his eyes against the slick guilt writhing through him. He knew he had taken advantage of her. She had been sweetly innocent and he had used her, just like he used everyone else.

He drew in a ragged breath. "East. Why didn't you tell me?"

Her mouth wobbled a little, then tightened. "How was I supposed to do that?" She spoke in a low voice that damned him with every word. "You left in the morning before I was even awake. It was obvious you couldn't stand to be near me anymore."

No. Oh no. How could she even think that? He had held her as the sky began to turn pink with dawn and had known he couldn't stay. They had no future together. She was sweet and innocent, generous and giving. After five years embroiled in his world of lies and betrayals after he was recruited, he couldn't even endure his own company, forget about asking her to do the same.

"Not true," he growled. "It wasn't you."

She didn't look convinced. "I wanted to tell you. I would have, if I'd known how to reach you. For months after, even Jo didn't know where you were."

He had been deep undercover at the time and had barely managed to squeeze away for Guff's funeral. Afterward, he had buried himself in work again to forget his grief for his foster father and then his guilt over Easton and what he had done.

None of this seemed real and he couldn't seem to work his brain around it. They had a child together. A son.

"Why didn't Jo tell me? Why didn't *anyone* tell me?"

"Nobody else knew."

She sighed and sat on the snow crook again, gazing at the lake that bubbled and danced in the breeze.

"Remember when I took that job with the cattlemen's association in Denver? I knew I couldn't stay here. Jo would have loved me and the baby and she would have…understood. But I wasn't sure about Brant and Quinn."

His foster brothers would have killed him for hurting Easton. No, they would have carved him into a thousand tiny pieces and *then* they would have killed him.

"So you thought you were protecting me?"

"No. I thought I was doing what was best for my… for my baby."

Questions swirled around inside his head. He couldn't

seem to focus on any of them. He slid to the ground and leaned back against the aspen trunk.

"I don't understand any of this, East. What happened? Was he…did someone adopt him?"

Her expression wobbled again and a tiny tear trickled down the side of her slim nose and suddenly he didn't want to hear the rest. He wanted to bury his face in his hands and pretend none of this was happening. *Had* happened.

She didn't answer for a long time. When she did, her voice was low, subdued. "I looked into adoption. But in the end, I couldn't do it. He was part of… I just couldn't. I loved him already."

She drew in a deep, shuddering breath. "He was… When I was eight months along, he stopped moving. It was a few hours before I realized it and…by the time I made it to the hospital, he was already gone. They induced labor but…it was too late."

His gut twisted and he raked a hand through his hair, devastated to think of Easton having to go through all this by herself.

"I named him Chance, even though he never really had one." Her voice was a little stronger now, but he still heard the grief threading through her words. "He's buried in Denver. I would have liked to bring him home to Pine Gulch, but I didn't know how without telling Jo and the others everything."

"And this?" he gestured to the plaque.

"After I came home, I needed somewhere I could come to remember him and those months when I carried him and…and loved him." She gave a ghost of a smile. "I think Guff would have forgiven me for borrowing a tree."

He wanted to go to her, to pull her into his arms and hold her close while he tried to absorb the shock and the pain and hurt raging through him.

He didn't know what to do with all these emotions, so he focused on the anger. "You've seen me since then. Maybe not often but sometimes. You should have told me. I had a right to know. How could you keep this from me, all these years?"

She inhaled sharply and rose to stand over him, her eyes glittering. "When you've carried a child by yourself for eight months, then labored for six hours to deliver a baby you already know is dead, you can lecture me about what I should and shouldn't have done."

"Easton…"

She stalked away from him toward her horse. He climbed to his feet and stood frozen for just a moment before he went after her, grabbing her hand before she could swing herself into the saddle.

"I'm sorry. This is… I never in a million years could have imagined this. You never said a single word, all this time. Can you blame me for being shocked? You've had five years. I've had five minutes to adjust to the fact that I've lost a son I never even knew I had."

She released a shuddering little breath and then turned back to him. Her body was tight and angry, but he thought he saw a slight softening in her eyes.

"Do you want to know why I didn't tell you?"

He nodded.

"Everything was already different between us after that night. Whenever you did come back, you couldn't even stand to look at me. I was afraid to tell you about

Chance. If I did, I thought you might never come back, and Jo…Jo needed you here as much as possible while she was sick."

"East. It wasn't you," he repeated. "I couldn't risk being near you because I didn't trust myself. I've known something was wrong all these years. I was just afraid to push because I assumed you were angry with me."

Could he feel any more selfish? She had been hurting, carrying this immense burden by herself, and he had focused only on himself and his own guilt. "I'm so sorry, Easton."

He couldn't bear this space between them another moment. He stepped forward and wrapped his arms around her, half fearing she would push him away and he would have to let her.

She stood frozen for a moment in his arms and then she let out a gasping sob and then another and he felt her slender frame shake and her arms wrap tightly around his waist.

He pressed his face to the soft, sweet curve of her neck and absorbed her sobs inside him. They stood wrapped together for a long time while the horses nickered softly in the distance and the breeze whispered through the aspens.

When he finally lifted his face, he knew something fundamental had changed between them.

"I'm so sorry I didn't know," he said hoarsely. "I'm so sorry you went through that by yourself. I wish you had told me."

She shifted so she could meet his gaze. "What would you have done? If I had been able to contact you when I first found out I was pregnant, would you have come back?"

The question hung between them, stark and unadorned. He didn't know how to answer. He thought of the dark and ugly place he had been in his life back then, the difficult choices he had been forced to make.

"Would you have wanted me to?" he asked, instead of giving her a direct answer.

Her mouth trembled. "Yes. I wanted you here every single moment of every day. I still do."

He stared at her, stunned by her vehemence. He didn't know what to say and so he did the only thing he could think of. He slid his arms around her and pulled her close.

Chapter Ten

She seemed too slight and fragile in his arms, as if the tiniest breath might shatter her into tiny shards.

He knew it was an illusion. She wasn't fragile. She was the toughest woman he knew. She ran the entire ranch by herself, gave orders to the men, could drive a massive John Deere with her eyes closed.

And she had endured more pain than he could imagine. His throat felt tight and achy when he thought of her going through a pregnancy alone, away from everyone she loved and everything she knew.

He could picture her swelling with his child, talking to him, singing to him.

Loving him.

She must have been lonely as hell—not to mention scared to death—living in Denver by herself. He couldn't believe she had kept her pregnancy a complete secret to everyone and hadn't even told Jo.

He could have spared her that. If he hadn't run off like an idiot, so full of himself and what he was doing, he might have spared a minute or two to think about the consequences of their night together.

And then she had to endure the ultimate pain of losing their child by herself, while he was off wading through muck and misery, trying to save the world.

Would he ever be able to live with the guilt of that? Probably not. The only thing he could do now was offer what comfort he could provide, which seemed pitifully meager. He pressed his forehead to hers, his heart aching with the weight of a torrent of emotions: sadness, tenderness, the overwhelming rightness of being here with her.

Maybe he would have been content with that, with holding her close in shared sorrow for their child. But she brushed her lips against his, once, twice, then again.

It seemed unbearably sweet to stand here kissing her with the mountain air shivering between them.

They stood that way for a long time wrapped together, the kiss slow and easy. Her arms twisted around his neck and she leaned closer to him. He could feel her lithe curves against him. His body stirred and he was suddenly painfully reminded of the heat that always simmered inside him when she was near.

He couldn't help it, he deepened the kiss, dancing his tongue along the seam of her mouth. She froze for just a heartbeat before she opened for him and leaned into his kiss.

Her response snapped apart the tight leash on his control. He groaned and pulled her closer, his blood a wild pulse in his ears.

All he could think about was how perfect she felt in his arms.

They kissed for a long time until he was beyond thought, far past reason, until he pressed her back against the tree trunk and her fingers tangled in his hair and his at the bare skin under her shirt, just above the waistband of her jeans.

She made tiny little sounds of arousal that turned him on more than anything he'd ever heard in his life and she pressed her soft curves more tightly to him. Tenderness and hunger and emotions he didn't want to face twisted around inside him and he was just sliding his thumbs up her rib cage when, through the haze of awareness that surrounded them, the high, distinctive screech of a red-tailed hawk pierced the afternoon.

One of the horses whinnied in response and at the sound, Cisco froze, jerked sharply back to awareness.

What the hell was he doing? He eased his mouth away and stared at her, his breathing ragged and every nerve ending on fire for her.

Her eyes were wide, her lips swollen. Self-doubt coiled through him, as sharp as barbed wire.

He was an animal. A filthy, rutting beast. After everything she had just told him, how could he treat her like she was one of the eager cantina girls?

He slid his hands away and stepped back a pace.

"I'm sorry. Damn. I'm so sorry."

Her color was high and her hand trembled as she tucked a loose strand of hair behind her ear, but somehow she managed a cool look out of eyes that were still red from her crying earlier. "Sorry for what? Returning a kiss I started?"

His body burned for her and he couldn't even look at

her without having to fight the powerful urge to yank her back into his arms, to plunder that soft, delicious mouth again. To kiss away every trace of tears.

"I have no right."

"Why not?"

"It's not…you're not…"

"What, Cisco? Because we basically grew up together? Or because of…because of Chance?"

"All those reasons." And more. He would only bring her more unhappiness and she had already suffered enough, damn it.

He screwed his eyes shut. She deserved so much better. She deserved a man who could protect her, who could make her happy. A man who could sleep at night.

"What about Bowman? I thought you were dating him." He was grasping for straws and he had a feeling they both knew it.

She shook her head. "Trace is a great guy. But he's not you."

She stepped forward, her eyes a soft, stunning blue. "I wanted you to kiss me, Cisco. I wanted you to kiss me five years ago, I wanted you to kiss me when you came back three days ago."

She paused and despite everything, heat curled through him when he saw the tiny smile playing at the corners of her mouth.

"And I want you to kiss me again now," she whispered.

She moved across the space he had created between them, until her high, firm breasts were touching his chest.

"Kiss me, Cisco," she murmured, her breath soft and sweet against his mouth.

What else could he do but obey?

He groaned and closed his eyes for just a moment before he lowered his mouth to hers.

Finally.

Oh.

Finally. She shivered as he deepened the kiss, as his arms pulled her tightly against his hard strength.

Even with the lingering sadness that twined around and between them—their shared sorrow over both Belle and little Chance—she wanted to savor this moment.

He was here in her arms again, after all the years she had spent without him, and she wasn't about to waste an instant. She closed her eyes, surrendering to the wonder, to the taste and scent and feel of him.

His mouth trailed from her mouth to the pulse that fluttered at the base of her throat and then back up to just below her ear. She twisted her fingers in his hair, unbearably aroused as he licked and tasted her skin.

His hands moved to the buttons of her shirt and her knees wobbled as his hand covered one lacy cup of her bra. When his thumb slid the cup aside and teased her nipple, her thigh muscles shook and she sagged against him.

"We can't do this here," he growled, and she realized they still stood together in the meadow near the lake. Her gaze fell on the small shelter twenty yards away and with a sweet sense of the inevitable, she gripped his fingers and tugged him toward it.

The shelter was too humble even to be called a cabin, only four bare walls and a roof, but this was where they had spent their one and only night wrapped in each other's arms and she had always loved it for that reason alone.

She came here sometimes in her weaker moments and she kept blankets and pillows in an old metal critter-proof trunk for those moonlit trips to the lake she still sometimes managed to steal.

Cisco watched her, his eyes hooded, as she released the trunk latch and lifted the lid. The sweet summer scent of lavender drifted up from the sachets she had slipped inside the last time she was here.

She pulled out two soft, worn quilts and spread them on the wood floor. Then, nerves still fluttering through her, she smiled at Cisco.

"Are you sure?" he asked, his voice low, intense. "After everything, are you sure?"

"Kiss me," she demanded again and everything inside her seemed to shiver and sigh with delight when he finally complied.

For five years, she had relived the night they spent together hundreds of times. She thought nothing could compare to the heat and the magic of it.

As he touched her again, his hands warm on her bare skin, she discovered her memory was a pale shadow compared to the reality. She had forgotten the silky taste of his mouth and the scent of him, musky and male. She had forgotten the soul-wrenching intensity of his touch, of his warm skin against her. She had forgotten the delicious hunger thrumming inside her and his consummate skill at building it ever higher.

They kissed and touched for a long time, relearning each other's bodies, until they were both breathing heavily. He was battered and bruised, this man she loved so desperately. She was careful of his recent injury, but she could see in the slanting afternoon light that he had others. A puckered scar here, a jagged one there.

Despite his scars, he was beautiful, wild and masculine. She was especially drawn to the compass rose tattoo on his forearm, intricate and old-fashioned like something off a Renaissance sea captain's charts. It might have been a symbol of a wandering man, but somehow she sensed it meant more, that it was somehow connected to here and to the bond between Jo's Four Winds.

She trailed her mouth down and pressed her lips to the center of it and when she lifted her gaze to his, the heat in his dark eyes scorched down every nerve ending. He growled her name and leaned over her, twisting her so her body was under his.

His hands gripped hers and he kissed her with a raw concentration that took her breath away. He kissed her until she was trembling and weak, until her body shifted restlessly against him. Finally, when she didn't know how she could endure another moment, he slid between her thighs and entered her.

She clutched him to her, burning the moment and the memory into her mind. Her throat ached with the words of love she had carried inside her for so long, but she couldn't say them. Not here. Not now.

Not yet.

Instead, she showed him with her body, with her touch, with her kiss. His mouth found hers and she sighed his name against his mouth and then gasped as he reached between them to touch and tease her.

She held back her climax as long as she could, desperate to savor every second with him, but finally the heat and the hunger roared out of her control. The world blurred around her and on a ragged cry, she found release.

When she came back to awareness several seconds later, she found him watching her with brown eyes that blazed with emotions she couldn't read.

"You're so beautiful, East. The most beautiful thing I've ever seen."

He kissed her fiercely, his mouth hard and demanding, and she arched to meet him until a moment later his body went taut as he found his own release.

He fell asleep almost at once. Even though his eyes were closed and his breathing even, she still sensed tension in him, as if his muscles were coiled and ready for trouble at any moment. Her heart grieved for the life he must live and she wanted fiercely to soothe him.

Acting on instinct, she slid her arm across his chest above the white bandage and curled it over him, nestling against his side.

"East," he breathed softly, pulling her closer. He didn't open his eyes and she was almost positive he hadn't awakened. Still, his arm tightened around her and some of the tension seemed to ease from his features.

She had to tell him the rest. She sighed as nerves fluttered through her like the azure butterflies out in the meadow.

The words she hadn't been able to say in the heat of the moment, as it were, pressed hard to be spoken. She had to tell him how very much she loved him. Chances were, he still wouldn't be willing to accept the gift, but she had to offer it to him just the same.

Would she have the nerve, knowing she could be

risking everything? Or would she chicken out, as she had done the night before.

If she revealed just how deeply her feelings ran, she might be left with not even his infrequent visits and rare e-mails.

A tiny, fretful part of her urged her to stay silent. Better a few morsels than nothing at all, right?

She sighed. No. She had to tell him. She knew she would never be free of this love in her heart that she had lived with since she was a girl. But Trace had been right, she had been tightly clutching the barest thread of hope that perhaps Cisco might some day stop wandering.

Her fingers traced his forearm and the intricate compass ink there. That meant something. She knew it did. Even when he was far away, he had kept this connection to his home, always within his sight.

She would tell him. Not right now, but soon, she promised herself.

Until then, she would savor the miraculous gift of these few moments with him, even if that was all she would ever have.

She awoke some time later to a completely unaccustomed languorous sense of well-being. Her muscles felt loose and comfortable and she wasn't sure she could move, even if she wanted to.

The air had cooled slightly, but underneath the blanket, absorbing all his body heat, she didn't feel the chill.

She blinked her eyes open and found Cisco lying beside her, his gaze intent on her features.

"Hey." She smiled but felt a tiny chill sneak through

her when he didn't smile back. Instead, something haunted and dark flickered in his eyes.

No. She wouldn't let him ruin this with stupid, pointless regrets. She had dreamed of this for far too long. Since she didn't know what else to say or do, she wrapped her arm around his neck and pulled him down to her. At least when he was kissing her, he wasn't thinking about all the reasons why he shouldn't.

When her lips brushed his, she tasted his reluctance, but she refused to let him surrender to it. She kissed him softly, tenderly.

"This is good between us, Cisco. Why won't you trust me?"

"You're not the one I don't trust," he answered, a ragged edge to his voice.

"Trust this, then," she answered and deepened the kiss with a wild, almost desperate passion. His hesitance lasted only a moment, and then he made that sexy low sound in his throat and returned the kiss and she felt his body rise to join hers.

Both of them stayed awake after the second time they made love. Easton didn't want to waste any more of their precious time together with something as mundane as sleep when she could be savoring each moment with him.

"Are you hungry?" he asked, his fingers tugging the end of her disheveled braid. "I made a couple of sandwiches before I rode out after you."

She was touched that he would think of it, especially since she hadn't eaten much breakfast, too upset over Belle's impending departure The reminder of the baby sobered her and her heart gave a sharp twinge. How was she? Had she fallen asleep on the drive? Had they reached her new home in Boise yet?

She couldn't think about that right now either.

"I *am* hungry, now that you mention it."

"Why don't we get dressed, then, and we can sit by the lake and eat?"

Do we have to? she wanted to ask. *Why can't we just stay here and pretend the rest of the world and all the pain and heartache down the mountain doesn't exist?*

Impossible, she knew. Eventually they would have to return to real life. After a moment, she slipped out of his arms and reached for her clothing as he did the same. She pulled on her jeans and was buttoning her shirt when Cisco winced as he pulled on his own shirt.

The bandage around his abdomen was stark against his bronze skin, one too many secrets between them and she suddenly couldn't bear it.

"What really happened to you?" she demanded.

He looked up, his fingers on the buttons of his shirt. "What do you mean?"

She gestured to the wide bandage. "I'm not stupid, Cisco. I know you didn't get stabbed in a bar fight."

His mouth hardened and his expression grew shuttered. "What reason would I have to lie to you?"

"You tell me." It hurt, more than she wanted to acknowledge, that he would deflect her questions now, after the heat and magic they had just shared.

She had to know suddenly. For once, couldn't they have a dratted conversation without all the thick layers of subtext?

"Who pulled a knife on you? What were you doing?

Why are you so determined to keep your life some big, spooky secret from me?"

He said nothing for a few moments. A magpie squawked at them from outside, then he shifted his attention to the buttons of his shirt. "Listen to me. You're better off in the dark on this one, East."

She couldn't bear his damned evasions anymore. After everything—the revelation about Chance, the sweet peace of their lovemaking, all the tenderness she had tried to pour into her kisses—why couldn't he just tell her the truth?

"I'm not nine years old anymore, some stupid little girl you have to protect from the world. I'm a woman. And not just any woman either. I'm the woman who gave birth to your child. Who buried him alone. I have the right to know who you are, don't you think? Earlier you basically said you trust me. Why won't you trust me with this?"

She stood in front of him so he had no choice but to look at her, to meet her gaze. "Are you in trouble with the law? Trace seems to think you are."

A muscle flexed in his jaw, but she wasn't sure if that was in reference to any wrongdoing on his part or her mention of the police chief.

He seemed to be waging some internal struggle and she wasn't sure which side won when he walked out of the shelter toward the lake's edge, where Guff had years ago erected a bench, situating it at the perfect angle to take in the granite mountains and the shimmering, silvery water.

Cisco seemed oblivious to the pristine setting. He sat down heavily, his features closed and his eyes murky.

She sat beside him, waiting for him to wrestle whatever demons her question had stirred in him.

"Jo loved this spot," she said after several moments, sensing he needed more time. "Remember that?"

"Yeah," he said gruffly.

She smiled a little at a sudden bittersweet memory. "She came here just a week or so before she died. It was the night of the harvest moon and she would not rest until she had been able to enjoy one more moonlit ride. By that point, she could barely hold her head up anymore, but she made Tess and Quinn bring her up here. Quinn rode double with her the whole way, holding her on."

Quintessential Jo, determined to wring every drop of joy out of her life even as it faded away. Easton felt extraordinarily blessed in her life to been given the love and example of two strong women—her mother and her aunt. She wondered what they would have done in her situation, how they would feel about the choices she had made.

"I was knifed by a Colombian drug cartel boss," Cisco said abruptly, his words clattering between them like a rockslide down the mountain. "I'm a mid-level drug dealer."

Chapter Eleven

Whatever she expected him to say, that wasn't it. She inhaled sharply and for one brief moment, her insides seemed to shrivel with shock and dismay.

No. As quickly as her exhaled breath, reason and good sense and all her instincts intruded.

He was lying. She didn't know why, but she knew without any trace of doubt that his words weren't the truth.

The assurance was warm, comforting. Whatever he was involved with, she *knew* Cisco. She knew his heart and she knew he wasn't the sort of man who would profit off other people's misery.

She had always known he couldn't be doing anything like that, she realized. She just hadn't trusted her own instincts and hadn't allowed herself to trust *him*.

She shifted on the bench to face him. Acting on instinct, she reached for his arm, the one with the compass rose, and held it in her hands. "No, you're not. Now tell me the truth."

An arrested expression flickered across his features. "How do you know that *isn't* the truth."

"Because I know you. The real you. This persona you've been creating these last few years, that you're some kind of shiftless wanderer, isn't real. I don't know why you've perpetuated it, but I know it's an illusion. You're good and decent, Cisco. The kind of man who rushes back to his dying foster mother's bedside, no matter how much effort or cost it takes, the kind who steps up to care for an orphaned little girl even when he's injured himself. The kind who cries for a child he never even knew."

He gazed at her for a long time, his eyes a deep, glittery brown in the sunlight reflected off the water. Finally his other hand reached for hers and they sat close together while the wind rippled tiny waves on the lake and the mountain breeze whispered in the trees.

"I *am* a mid-level drug dealer," he finally said.

"Cisco—"

"Or at least that's been my cover on and off for the last decade. Among other things." His fingers tightened on hers. "I shouldn't be telling you this, Easton. It's too dangerous."

"You haven't told me anything yet."

He sighed reluctantly. "I'm an undercover federal agent. Narcoterrorism, mostly."

Of course. She closed her eyes. *Of course!*

So many things made sense now. His secrecy, the haunted shadows in his gaze, the difficulty she and the others had in finding him in an emergency. She should have realized long ago and she felt supremely stupid for not picking up all the clues.

Her mind sorted through details of the past and she realized Brant and Quinn probably suspected something of the sort all along.

"Why didn't you tell me?" she whispered. "All these years Jo and I were sick with worry for you. You seemed to drift farther away from here with every passing year."

"You were right to worry." His voice was hard, cold. "It's a hell of a life. A good agent becomes his cover. Yeah, you can cloak it in high and mighty words like the greater good and all that bull. But the harsh truth is, I'm a drug dealer. An arms dealer. And sometimes worse. Whatever I need to be. I've had to do...terrible things. The end result might get a few higher-level thugs out of the game, but good people are usually hurt in the process. People like John and Socorro Moore. Like Belle, who now has to grow up without her parents."

Her heart ached for the little girl with the huge eyes and the happy smile.

"Her parents worked with you?"

Something harsh and bleak swept over his features like a January canyon wind. "John did, anyway. He was one of the best. Smart, resourceful, intuitive. Until a cocaine cartel boss named *El Cuchillo* got hold of him and started to suspect he wasn't all he pretended to be. Before he finally died, John was tortured for a week by that psychopath, but he refused to give up his partner. Me."

She twisted her fingers around his and pressed her cheek against his shoulder.

"And Soqui?"

"They were so in love. John secretly married her when he found out she was pregnant with Belle, even though it compromised everything we knew and broke about a dozen agency rules. They were happy together in whatever tiny furtive minute they could steal together."

He paused. "I used to hate seeing them together. Nothing makes you feel more alone than being with two people who are crazy about each other."

She flashed him a quick look, but he appeared to regret the revealing words because he quickly continued. "I knew it couldn't end well. John knew it, too, I think. In his distraction, he started to get a little careless. Somehow he slipped up and *Cuchillo* began to suspect he was wrong."

His hand curled into a fist. "After John died, Soqui insisted on playing a part in taking down the man who killed him. I tried to tell her it wasn't a good idea. She had Belle to think about. But she was determined and since she already had an in because she was childhood friends with *Cuchillo's* woman, my concerns were overruled by…others."

He sighed. "We worked together for several months while Belle was hidden away in a safehouse outside Bogotá. We had enough evidence a hundredfold to extradite *Cuchillo,* but we were working on the players in the level above him."

"What happened?"

"Somehow our cover was blown. I still don't know how. Maybe the girlfriend, maybe Soqui let something slip. I just know on the night I was supposed to be there for a huge buy, *El Cuchillo* and three of his soldiers ambushed us at the warehouse. I took out the thugs but not before one of them gut-shot Soqui. I went to help her, but *El Cuchillo* turned on me with a knife, his trademark calling card. That's what *cuchillo* means. Knife. He carried a ten-inch blade in this stupid little scabbard on his belt. I was expecting him to come at me, but because I was concerned for Soqui, I moved a hair too slowly."

He was silent, gazing out at the lake, where the trout and arctic graylings were beginning to jump for their evening meal.

"What happened to him?" she finally asked.

He slanted her a long, dark look and she would have shivered if not for the warmth of his body next to hers. The man was dead. She didn't need Cisco to answer for her to understand clearly.

So many things made sense now, she thought again. No wonder he slept with a handgun under his pillow, why he seemed alert and ready at all times, as dangerous as a crouched mountain lion. Because he had to be.

"You feel responsible for Soqui's death. That's why you brought Belle back to John's family."

"I *am* responsible."

"How? You just said yourself that you fought against her being involved in the investigation in the first place."

"But I didn't try hard enough to stop it. I knew we could get deeper in with her help than without, so I used her, just like everyone else. I…sensed something was off that night, but I was too blinded by the chase. I wanted it over, so she could go back to being a mother to Belle. I was so invested in taking down *Cuchillo* and the bastards who pulled his strings that I lost all perspective, didn't trust my gut."

She couldn't imagine his world, the pressure and the tension and the danger. Her life here running a busy cattle ranch seemed staid and pale in comparison. "Why didn't you tell me?" she asked again.

He absently scratched at Jack's ears. "I just gave you a tiny portion of what my life is like. It's ugly and dark. Better that you think I'm some irresponsible drunken beach bum. Safer for you."

She stared at him. "In what alternate universe would that possibly be better? You're a hero, Cisco."

"I'm no hero," he growled. "I lie, I steal, I sell drugs that ruin people's lives. Didn't you hear me? I kill people."

He truly believed that, she realized. He could only see the ugliness, not the end result of what he did.

"You're walking directly into the darkness so you can push it back a little for the rest of us, Cisco. To make the world a little safer for people like me. What else would you call someone willing to do that but a hero?"

He said nothing for a long moment, but she could tell by the stunned look in his eyes that her words had struck something inside him.

Sensing he needed time to absorb her words and her faith in him, she squeezed his fingers again and stood up,

"I suppose we had better start heading back," she said, though she wanted nothing so much as to stay here in the quiet peace of the alpine lake. "My animals will be hungry for dinner. We never did get to the picnic you spent so much time fixing."

"Right."

He rose and helped her gather the blankets and return them to the trunk inside the shelter. A short time later, they headed down the trail with Jack in the lead, scouting for any small mammals unlucky enough to choose that particular afternoon to cross his path.

Cisco rode behind her on the narrow trail and said little. She imagined that, like her, he was wrung out by the emotional storm of the afternoon.

Trace's words echoed in her head. *Tell him how you feel. See if he might feel the same.*

She was going to have to do it, to hand him everything in her heart. How would she ever find the courage? she wondered, then was ashamed of herself. If he had the courage to face what he did day after day, couldn't she swallow her fears to utter a few simple words?

The image of Jo riding up this trail in the moonlight with Quinn and Tess, seizing every moment of her life even as her strength dwindled, flashed through her mind. Jo had found the courage for this, for one last chance to see a place she loved.

Easton felt the strangest sense of urgency, as if—like Jo seeing her last harvest moon—she had one final chance to help Cisco preserve whatever pieces of himself he had left after ten years of pretending to be something and someone else.

He desperately needed the peace of the ranch and, perhaps, of her love. She owed it to both of them to do everything she could to provide that to him.

No matter how terrifying she found it to tell him everything in her heart.

* * *

One more night.

He would allow himself one last gift of a few precious hours with her before he slithered back to the lies and the ugliness.

Yeah, it was selfish of him, he knew. He had already hurt her, more than he could ever have imagined. He thought of that plaque on the tree, of her slender form growing larger with a child she would never hold.

An altruistic, noble guy—somebody like Brant, for instance—would just keep riding, would probably go straight from unsaddling Russ to climbing into his rental car so he could drive out of her life for good.

But he was a selfish son of a bitch and he wanted a few more hours with the woman he...

With Easton.

He couldn't say it. Couldn't even think of it. She was Easton, his center, his touchstone, his heart. He didn't deserve to love her, not after all he had done.

He touched his thumb to the *E* on his compass rose tattoo as he rode, barely aware he was even doing it. The trees opened up as they neared the ranch and he could see it there in the long shadows of late afternoon. The sprawling ranch house, the neat fence lines, the barn and outbuildings.

The tug inside him had nothing to do with his knife wound. He might still be afraid to face his true feelings for her after all these years, but he would readily admit how he felt about this place. He loved Winder Ranch and had a deep and powerful yearning for the peace and serenity he found here.

When they reached the barn, Suzy came out to greet them. Well, to greet Jack, anyway. She barked a greeting, tail wagging, then rushed to lick her mate's snout like he was a soldier returning from war.

He saw Easton give the pair a soft smile as she slid down from her horse.

"Want to help me with chores?" she asked him.

He wanted to spend every moment with her that he could until he left again, even if that meant mucking out stables and hauling hay around a knife injury.

"Sure," he answered. "I'll start with the horses."

For the next hour, they worked together feeding and watering the stock. After the thick emotions of the day—the sadness of saying goodbye to Belle and then the shock and grief he still hadn't fully absorbed at learning of the baby they had lost and, of course, the sweet tenderness of having her in his arms again—he would never have expected they could be so relaxed together.

She made him laugh a half-dozen times when their paths would cross as they worked, with her funny observations about the animals, about her ranchhands, about her memories of all the ways he and the other boys found to avoid an excess expenditure of energy on labor whenever they could.

She made the work fun and inspired him to try harder, which he had always considered one of her particular gifts.

When he finished the list of embarrassingly mild chores she gave him, he realized he was alone in the barn. When he went in search of her, he found her with her crossed arms propped on the top fence railing around the horse pasture, watching the half-dozen animals graze in the soft, backlit glow of gathering twilight.

"I love this time of day," she said, sensing his presence even before he reached her side. "When the work is almost done and the animals are all settling down and everything is quiet and still."

She lifted her face to the lavender sunset edging the mountains. She was so beautiful, like sunshine and wildflowers, and she made his throat ache.

"You're lucky to be able to see it every day," he said, his voice hoarse. "Trust me, there are very few places on earth that compare to the peace here."

She gave him a long, steady look before she shifted her attention back to the horses. "Why don't you stay, then?"

"Easton..."

"Just shut up for a minute, would you, and listen to me. Really listen. Before you give me all the noble reasons why you have to go, why you have obligations, why your work is important, blah blah blah, *think* about it. You're happier here than anywhere else. This is your home, Cisco. You've given years of your life. Don't you deserve a little peace?"

"It's not that simple."

"Sure it is. Whoever you work for can get by without you. You're not singlehandedly holding back the darkness, Cisco. Can't you trust the job to someone else for a while?"

Chapter Twelve

She held her breath, unable to read anything in his eyes. Was he shocked, angry, exasperated? She couldn't tell from his expression and it took every ounce of courage she could summon to turn to him, to raise her arms and wrap them around his neck.

"Stay here with me, Cisco. Help me run the ranch."

Now she saw emotion in his eyes. They were dark, anguished and soaked with regret. "I ca—"

She couldn't bear his answer. Not now, after all that they had shared. To stop the words, she pressed her mouth to his and swallowed them inside her. He stood frozen for a heartbeat and then he kissed her back with a fierceness that bordered on desperation.

She didn't know whether to be afraid at his response or heartened. He cared for her. She knew he did. If he didn't, would he kiss her as if she were his very salvation?

The sun was sliding over the crest of the mountains when she eased away from him. The air seemed to have already turned cooler. A couple of the younger horses raced through the pasture, manes and tails flying, and a pair of meadowlarks trilled their evening tune.

He was so warm, she wanted to burrow in and stay there forever, but she forced herself to ease away. "Before you make any decision about…about the future, you need to know something else. Something I should have told you years ago."

He watched her silently, warily, and she drew in a shaky breath with a last prayer for courage.

"I'm in love with you," she whispered.

His eyes widened with shock even as his jaw hardened. "You're not."

"Wanna bet?" She tilted her head and studied him, wondering if his surprise could actually be genuine. "Come on, Cisco. You must have had some idea. I was a virgin five years ago. Why did you think I waited if it wasn't for you?"

She rarely saw him at a loss for words, even when he was a kid, but just now her fast-talking, smooth Cisco looked completely disconcerted. "I don't know. I just… I guess I figured you just hadn't been that serious with anybody yet. Not for lack of trying on the guys' part, I'm sure."

"I dated other guys. But none of them was you," she said simply. "I've been in love with you since the day you showed up at Winder Ranch, Cisco. You were skinny and ragged and I could see you were scared, but you grinned at us all like you owned the place and that was it for me. I knew *you* were it for me."

She didn't miss the flare of panic on his features, the almost imperceptible distance he moved away from her. In her secret fantasies, she supposed she had hoped he would sweep her into his arms, declare his undying love and his wish never to be separated from her.

But life wasn't a fairy tale. She had learned that in a hospital delivery room in Denver as she held the tiny, blanket-wrapped form of their child.

She should stop now, before she ruined everything between them, but she had come this far. She wouldn't back down now.

"I love you, Cisco. Not the way I love Brant and Quinn. They were always like big brothers to me. My feelings for you were always different. Somewhere inside you, I know you sensed that and felt the same."

He had felt the sparks between them. She knew he had. Even before her uncle's funeral, heat had simmered between them and he would have to be lying if he tried to deny it.

"I love you," she repeated, praying if she said it enough times he might start believing her. "I loved being pregnant with Chance. Even though I was alone and afraid, it was…a magical time, knowing I would have part of you, no matter what."

His features were stony and remote. She might have thought he was unmoved by what she said, except for the death grip he had on the top railing of the pasture fence.

"Easton, I…" His voice trailed off and her heart sank. She had lost him. Even when he said nothing else, she knew he was firmly closing the door she had tried so hard to open.

Tears stung her eyes, but she focused on the horses until she could regain some semblance of control.

She could be tough. She had survived a mother's ultimate pain—losing her child. She could survive losing her baby's father, too, although right at this moment she wasn't entirely certain of that.

Still, she forced a smile. "You don't have to say anything right now, Cisco. Just think about what I've said, okay? Ask yourself if you're really happy where you are. You've done this for a long time. Maybe it's time to let somebody else carry that burden for a while."

She decided not to wait for him to answer, since she was almost certain she wouldn't like what he had to say.

"We never did get those sandwiches," she said quickly. "I haven't eaten all day and I'm starving. Let's go find some dinner."

He opened his mouth to answer, but she didn't give him a chance, simply hurried back to the house.

He didn't come into the house until she had nearly finished broiling a couple of salmon fillets she'd taken out of the freezer a few days earlier and tossing a salad to go with them. Even though she knew it was only delaying the inevitable, she threw a determined effort into being cheerful during dinner, distracting him whenever he looked as if he wanted to say something serious.

After they finished eating and cleaned up the kitchen together, he suggested they go out to Jo's porch swing.

When she was seven years old, before any of the boys came, Easton broke her arm falling out of the big apple tree down behind the foreman's cottage. She had hid her pain from everyone, had pretended for two days that nothing was wrong because she didn't want to miss out on a planned camping trip up to the high country with her dad and Uncle Guff, until finally her mother had caught her crying in her room and she had finally confessed all.

This felt a great deal like that. She knew she was going to have to face the inevitable pain at some point, but not yet. She didn't want to ruin this moment with him and somehow she knew going to the porch swing with Cisco would provide him the opportunity to tell her he was leaving.

Her heart would hurt much more than any broken bone, she knew. But she wasn't ready to face that yet.

"I would rather stay in," she told him. She forced a smile and wrapped her arms around his neck and kissed him with a desperate intensity she knew he must sense.

He paused for only a moment and then he framed her face with his hands and kissed her back with a matching hunger.

Lovemaking apparently tired Easton out.

Later, after they came together with that same wondrous heat, she slid easily into sleep as if she was ten years old again, swinging into the hay pile in the barn with her braids flying out behind her.

Her head nestled on his shoulder, her luscious hair caressing his skin and her arm resting just above his stupid bandage.

He shifted so he could look at her and a torrent of emotions washed through him. More than anything, he wanted to stay right here in her bedroom, to keep the rest of the world at bay forever.

The world waited for him, though, dark and insistent.

He gazed up at the ceiling. Her words—the ones that had firmly lodged in his mind, in his heart—rang through his memory again.

I love you, Cisco.... Somewhere inside you, I know you sensed that and felt the same.

Stay here with me, Cisco. Help me run the ranch.

I have loved you since the day you showed up at the ranch.

What she asked was impossible. He had obligations. Delicate webs that had been spun months, even years before, that were only now ready to catch their prey.

How could he just walk away from everything?

He closed his eyes. He wanted to. Oh, how he wanted to. The urge to say yes was an urgent need under his skin, a fire coursing through his blood.

Impossible. She wouldn't want him here. Oh, she might say she was in love with him but she loved an illusion. A memory. He wasn't that skinny, fun-loving kid anymore. He hadn't been him in a long time.

Could he find that kid again, somewhere buried deep down?

The thought tantalized him. Only here was that even possible. Once he walked away from her this time and left the ranch, he somehow knew that tiny shred of himself would be gone for good.

If he stayed, he would let her down, though. She would discover he wasn't all those things she thought. He wasn't good or decent. He was a man willing to lie and use people to get what he wanted.

She would come to hate him eventually.

He was cold, suddenly, despite the warmth from her strong, slender body.

As she slept on, he watched her breathe, saw the shadow of her eyelashes on her cheekbones, the delicate curve of her mouth, the tiny smattering of freckles she hid during the day with makeup.

Even though he had been trained to be a consummate liar, his words to her earlier had been nothing less than the truth. She was the most beautiful woman he had ever known, as beautiful in her heart as she was on the outside.

He watched her for a long time, then finally eased away from her body and tucked the covers more snugly around her to compensate for taking away his body heat. She frowned a little in her sleep and shifted her body as if searching for him, but eventually she settled again.

After a moment, he pulled on his jeans and moved to the window. Out of habit, he touched the *E* on his compass tattoo as he gazed out at the dark, still ranch. The only movement was one of the big barn owls soaring through a splash of moonbeam before it landed soundlessly in the big maple on the edge of Jo's garden.

He could stay. Could take the precious gift she was offering him of her peace and her love.

But what if he screwed it up? His fingers moved over the rest of the compass. The W, the S. Even the N.

If he stayed and hurt her, shattered all her illusions about him as he knew he eventually would, he would lose not only Easton but also Brant and Quinn. His brothers. He would have nothing—no family, no home. No heart.

He couldn't take that risk. He knew she would be hurt for a while if he left, but that would be only a tiny measure of the pain he would bring her if he stayed.

He closed his eyes, already hating himself, then he turned away from the window and reached for his boots.

Chapter Thirteen

"You sure you're okay, missy?"

Easton gave her foreman a steely stare as she shoved on her work gloves. "Why wouldn't I be?"

Burt spat a mouthful of sunflower seed shells onto the ground. "Don't know. Your eyes are still redder'n a chicken's wattle."

"Allergies," she muttered.

"That don't explain why you ain't said two words all morning."

She glared at him, not at all in the mood to hear him tell her he told her so.

"Maybe I've got better things to do than sit around asking everybody about their feelings this morning, Dr. Phil."

He spat another wad of seeds into the dirt and gave her a look right back that made her feel about six years old. Guilt pinched at her. Burt wasn't to blame that she wanted to curl up right here in the dirt and bawl for the next year or two. None of this was his fault and she was wrong to take her pain and humiliation out on him.

When she had awakened to an empty bed in the early hours before dawn, she had known. Somehow she had known. At first she had been numb and then the pain had crashed over her like a tsunami, raw and violent, sweeping her feet out from under her and tugging her out to a great gaping sea of loss while her shattered dreams floated past.

She hadn't needed to search the house to know he was gone. There was an emptiness in the air, as if some vital energy had been sucked out of the house.

Despite every instinct, she had still somehow hung on to a fragile flutter of hope. She had rushed to the window, only to see the empty spot on the driveway where his rental car had been parked.

She had returned to the bed they had shared as if she were a hundred years old and had sat in the middle of the mattress, arms wrapped around her knees. And then the tears started. She had sobbed for a long, long time, until her head pounded and her stomach felt vaguely ill, until the first rays of sunlight sidled through the window.

She might still be there now if she hadn't heard Jo's voice echoing in her ears. "Keep moving, darlin'. You can get through anything, as long as you don't let yourself stop moving."

The ranch needed her. She had five hundred head of cattle who depended on her. For the last five days her attention had been diverted by an injured dark-eyed wanderer and a darling little girl.

No more. It was time to throw herself back into the ranch she loved, to let the rhythm and routine of the place soothe her battered spirit and calm her aching heart.

"Think I'll ride up and check on the sandbag situation by the creek. You and the boys all right down here?"

Burt gave her a careful look and she had to look away, unable to bear his pity. "Should be."

Easton nodded and headed for the barn. She supposed she could take the pickup or one of the ATVs and be there in half the time, but she wanted to saddle Lucky anyway, both for the comfort she always found on a horse and because the task would take longer that way, giving her more time to focus on something besides the unrelenting pain. She had a feeling she would be filling her days with more busywork than ever in the coming days.

Jack bounded up to join her and she watched his lithe form as he trotted ahead of the horse, sniffing in the bushes for any unsuspecting ground squirrels who hadn't learned their lesson the day before.

Yesterday had been sunny and bright, more like late June than mid-May. In typical fickle Idaho spring fashion, the weather had turned. The sky was dank and lifeless and the air seemed colder, heavy with the impending storm forecasters were warning would arrive later in the evening. She was grateful she had grabbed a denim jacket on the way out of the barn.

She supposed the change in the weather was appropriate, since it so accurately reflected her mood.

He was gone.

Her hands tightened on the reins.

In her heart, she had known he would be. Even as

he kissed her and held her, she had tasted the desperate edge to their embrace, could almost see his gaze shifting toward the door.

Jack suddenly scared up a ruffed grouse, who drummed his wings loudly as he took flight.

She watched him go, wondering how far he would fly and if he would be safe, then she turned her attention back to the trail. When she reached the crossroads where the trail split, one part of her yearned to head toward the lake. Even Jack seemed to think that was the direction she wanted to go. He was twenty feet ahead of her and her horse, well on his way toward the lake and she had to whistle to call him back.

A part of her desperately sought the peace she found there, to sit by the little memorial plaque to Chance and sob for a few days in what she knew would be a vain effort to purge this pain inside.

She refused to indulge the impulse. She had to go forward. The strong women in her life would have expected no less.

She rode to where the creek threatened to run over its banks. The sandbags seemed to be holding, she was relieved to see, and the water appeared to have crested. The creek was still running high, but the danger of flooding seemed to have passed.

Good. One less crisis in her life for now. She and Burt and the ranchhands had done what they could to protect the hay.

Too bad she hadn't worked as hard to protect her heart the moment she awoke in the early hours of the morning five days ago and found Cisco in her kitchen.

No. Just like the creek bed here, the channel in her

heart that belonged to Cisco had been carved years ago. She had been right to tell him everything. Now there were no more secrets between them, not even the furtive hopes she might have harbored somewhere deep inside that he was only waiting for her to say the words.

She had thrown her heart at his feet and had all but begged him to give up his wandering life for her.

For a few glittery moments there by the horse pasture and the long shadows of approaching twilight, she had seen something in his eyes, some tiny glimmer that hinted he wanted exactly what she did. He had held her and kissed her with aching tenderness and she had been certain he must care for her.

She still thought he did. But perhaps the pull of his other life was stronger than what she offered. He had left—and the worst part was, now she had no idea if he would ever return. By spilling everything, telling him the depth of her feelings, things between them were bound to be awkward now. How could they go back to even the strained politeness of the last five years, when he knew how deeply she loved him?

She had known it was a gamble and she had taken it anyway. Now she would just have to live with the consequences, only hope she hadn't managed to drive him from Winder Ranch permanently. This was still his home, even if he only visited rarely.

"Oh, Cisco," she murmured aloud. Although she had thought she had a firm hold on her emotions by now, her throat ached suddenly and her eyes burned.

No. She wasn't going to do this now. If she returned to the ranch with tearstains on her cheeks, Burt would give her that morose look and probably make one of the poor ranchhands follow her around all day to keep an eye on her so she didn't break down again.

She shifted her weight in the saddle and whistled for Jack, who had wandered far ahead of her and was barking at something.

She frowned when he didn't immediately respond. The trail curved around a rock outcropping and she couldn't see him from here. She sincerely hoped he hadn't run across a dratted skunk, although she wanted to think Jack knew better than to tangle with one of those. Wouldn't that be just what she needed today, the fun and excitement of cleaning up a skunk-doused dog?

A bit warily, she walked her horse down the trail farther. When she rounded the rocks, she narrowed her gaze. Jack barked at another rider coming up the trail, too concealed by the shadows from the trees on either side for her to identify.

Burt wasn't crazy about horses—he preferred his pickup truck whenever possible—and she couldn't imagine why he would send one of the ranchhands up after her, unless he was being a mother hen again and fretting about her.

Before she could call him back to her side, her border collie rushed to greet the horse and rider with an enthusiastic bark.

She shaded her eyes with her hand for a better look and suddenly her heart gave one hard thump in her chest at the glint of sunlight on slightly shaggy dark hair.

Impossible. It couldn't be.

Cisco left.

She had already started the grieving process for him, for heaven's sake. All morning, she had been telling herself she would survive this pain as she had endured all the rest. How on earth was she supposed to do that with him popping in and out of her life whenever the mood struck him?

She wanted to turn around and race back up the trail as fast as Lucky Star could take her. Either that, or slide out of the saddle, sit right there in the dirt and cry.

Instead, she drew in a deep breath, squared her shoulders and urged the horse forward.

She could handle this. If he was only coming to offer her a proper goodbye, she would be tough and resilient, like the crooked aspen she loved near Chance's memorial tree, which had survived its own storms, bent and forever altered but not broken.

Something about him seemed off somehow, but she still couldn't see him clearly because of the angle of the sun and the trees that shadowed him.

When they were roughly thirty feet apart, she heard a wholly unexpected sound—a giggly little laugh that definitely wasn't coming from Cisco.

Now she saw why Cisco's position on the horse had seemed odd, something she had apparently missed in her initial shock at seeing him.

He wasn't alone.

Russ was carrying two passengers—Cisco and someone else bundled in his arms, a darling little girl with pink overalls and dark curls.

In her shock, Easton jerked the reins and Lucky obediently stopped. For a long moment, she could only stare, her heart pounding fiercely and her hands beginning to shake.

What could it mean? He was here and so was Belle.

After the devastating emptiness she had known all morning, she didn't know quite what to think, what to say.

She was still reeling when he reached her. Lucky and Russ were close enough to bump noses in greeting.

"Apparently Belle likes horses." When he spoke, his voice was gruff. "She's laughed the whole ride without an ounce of fear. Good thing, right?"

She drew in a ragged breath. "I don't...what are you doing here?"

"Looking for you. Burt told us where you'd gone and I decided I couldn't wait at the ranch for you to come back."

"You left," she whispered. "You always leave."

His mouth tightened and she thought she saw something dark and almost anguished flicker in his expression and then it was gone.

"Your eyes are red," he murmured.

She looked away, wondering if she looked as lousy as she felt right now. "The grass pollen count must be off the charts," she muttered.

He gave her a long look but didn't argue. Instead, he slid carefully from Russ's back, still holding Belle. The baby immediately wriggled to try to get down so she could play in the dirt.

"In a minute, little bug," he said, his voice soft. "We have to talk to East first."

She wasn't sure she wanted to hear what he had to say. One part of her still wanted to wheel Lucky around and head deep into the mountains where he couldn't hurt her anymore.

Reluctantly, she slid from her horse and gave him

rein to start chewing the spring grasses that grew beside the trail. When Easton neared the pair of them, Belle gave a delighted squeal and leaned away from Cisco as she held her hands out in that imploring way she had of demanding to be held.

She didn't know what else to do, especially when seeing Belle only made her realize again how very much she had missed the little girl. Easton pulled off her rough leather gloves, shoved them in her back pocket and reached for her. As she did, her hands brushed Cisco's forearms and she almost wept at the instant heat that sparked between them just at that simple touch.

Belle seemed so perfect in her arms. Easton held her close and kissed her soft, sweet-smelling cheek. When she lifted her gaze, she found Cisco watching them intently.

"I don't understand. You left," she repeated hoarsely.

"Yeah, I did. I planned to catch the first flight to Miami and then on to Bogotá as soon as I could. I didn't know what else to do."

How about stay with the woman who loves you? she thought as his words sent fresh pain slicing through her.

"Yet here you are. And with Belle. What's going on?"

"I couldn't do it," he said simply. "I planned to catch a flight out of Pocatello, but when I got there, somehow I just kept on driving. I told myself it was the logical choice, that I'd have a better chance of catching a direct flight out of Boise than a smaller airport like Pokey. But by the time I reached Boise's city limits, I knew I wouldn't be getting on any plane. I knew what I had to do."

"Which was?"

"Instead of heading to the airport, I found Sharon Weaver's house. Poor woman. It was only seven in the morning when I showed up and she already had kids hanging off her and looked like she hadn't slept all night."

Easton imagined she didn't look much better, since she'd spent most of the night weeping for him.

Belle tugged at her braid and started to put it in her mouth until Easton pulled it free and out of her reach. Still, he didn't seem inclined to elaborate and finally she had to ask.

"What are you doing, Cisco?"

He took another step forward and she had nowhere to retreat, with the horses behind her. She suddenly couldn't look away from the warmth blazing from his dark eyes.

"What I should have done five years ago. Hell, what I should have done *ten* years ago. I want to come home, East."

Goose bumps spread at his words and her heart did a little leap of joy. She was afraid to trust his words, though, too wary of more pain that might be in store for her.

And then he reached a hand out and touched her cheek and everything hard and frightened inside her seemed to melt.

"I love you. I've loved you as long as I can remember. Last night, you told me you fell in love with me when I climbed out of the pickup truck with Guff. Guess what? I've got you beat by about five minutes, maybe.

I can still remember driving up the road with Guff and seeing you standing there by the house. The sunlight was dancing in your hair and you were grinning as you played with Guff's old dog and you were the most beautiful thing I had ever seen."

A tear leaked out before she could stop it. She wanted so desperately to believe him, to let these flutters of joy inside her break free. But she was so very afraid to hope.

"I love you, Easton. I want a home, a family, with you."

Another tear leaked out and he caught it with his thumb and then lowered his mouth to hers with aching tenderness. She tasted regret and sorrow and apology and she soaked up every drop.

She imagined this was how the flowers in Jo's garden felt when she finally remembered to water them after a July heat wave—relieved and joyful and desperately grateful that all was suddenly perfect with the world.

Belle giggled and reached a little hand up between them to make her presence known. Easton eased away from his mouth. "What about Belle?" she asked.

A faint wash of color heated his cheeks and he scratched the back of his neck. "Okay, I'll admit, I wasn't thinking very clearly about that. Um, I probably should have talked to you first before I stopped at her aunt's house. But that woman has her hands full, East. You saw how it was with her and all those kids. In a few months when she has one more, things will only get worse."

He twisted one of Belle's curls around his finger, earning her big, gummy smile.

He gave Easton a hesitant grin that reminded her

painfully of the boy he used to be. "I guess I was hoping I could convince you to continue the proud Winder tradition of opening your home and your heart to a couple of lost souls who desperately need them."

His gaze met hers and she felt more tears trickle out as his grin slid away, replaced by raw emotion. "Starting with me and with Belle."

This was a crossroads, just like the one that led to Windy Lake, she realized. He was waiting for her to decide whether to be guarded and wary, afraid of more pain along the journey, or whether to seize this chance to have everything she had ever dreamed about.

Could she trust that he wouldn't decide in a month or two that his feet were too itchy, that he wasn't cut out for the steady, quiet life she offered?

Belle gave one of her happy little squeals and beamed at Easton. She looked from the baby to Cisco, who watched her silently.

She had no choice, she realized. She loved them both fiercely. The trail ahead might be full of screes and slick patches, briars and rock falls, but what life wasn't? The alternative, while safe, would be bleak and desolate.

Ride on through, darlin'. She could almost hear Jo's voice in her ear.

A shadow of uncertainty slid across his features. "I should have talked to you about Belle first," he said again.

She shook her head and smiled at him, unable to contain the joy bursting through her.

"No. It's perfect."

He went still for a moment and then he smiled, looking younger and less hard than she'd seen him in years. He wrapped his arms around both her and Belle and

Easton couldn't contain a little sob of happiness as he kissed her again.

"I couldn't bear it, Cisco. All morning I didn't know how I would endure." She laughed a little, though she heard the echo of her pain. "I was thinking maybe I would just have to sell the ranch and chase after you."

"Not that. Never that. I'm only sorry it took me so long to drive to Boise and back."

"What did you tell Sharon?"

"That we both already adored Belle and I knew we could give her a good home here. She cried a bit, but then told me she knew John and Soqui would have wanted their daughter to grow up in a place filled with love."

Easton rested her head on his shoulder, unable to still believe this was real, that he was here, that he wanted to stay.

"You're going to have to marry me, you know."

How could it be possible to be so insanely, completely happy when she had been in the depths of despair just minutes ago?

"Am I?" she asked.

He laughed. "Damn right, unless you want Brant and Quinn to hang me up by my, uh, thumbs from the hay hook in the barn. You know they're going to insist we make it legal."

She studied him. "Are you worried about their reaction if we're together?"

He kissed her forehead. "I think they've probably just been waiting for me to finally figure out this is right where I belong."

"It always has been," she murmured.

He lifted Belle out of her arms, then slung his other arm over her shoulders and kissed the top of her head.

"Come on, then," he said with a smile that curled her toes and warmed her heart and settled all her fears. "Let's go home."

Epilogue

"Come on, honey. You've got to hold still for the picture."

"No. Doggies!"

Cisco hitched his daughter more tightly in his arms as she tried to slither to the ground toward where Suzy lay in a patch of sunlight with her new batch of puppies wriggling just like Belle.

They were apparently an irresistible attraction—and when Belle wanted something, she wouldn't stop pushing until she figured out a way to get it.

Standing beside him in a bright sundress that made her look as fresh and lovely as Jo's garden all around them, Easton kissed Belle's cheek and adjusted a curl. "You can see the doggies in a minute, honey, I promise. We have to take a quick picture first to remember our big day. Go on, Mimi. Take it. Hurry."

Brant's wife adjusted the focus of her camera lens,

then clicked it a few times while Cisco did his best to keep a firm hold on Belle.

Mimi adjusted her angle and fired off a few more shots, then moved in for a close-up. "It's kind of fun being on the other side of the camera for a change, especially with this perfect light right now. These are going to be fantastic."

"Thanks, Mimi." Easton smiled radiantly, something he really hoped Mimi could capture on the image. "It will be wonderful to have something to remember Belle's official adoption day," she said.

Adoption. The word still made him swallow, Belle was really their daughter now. A year after that insane trip from Bogotá to Cold Creek Canyon, he still couldn't quite believe it was real. Yet here she was in his arms, plump and busy and adorable.

And beside him stood his wife—that was another word that made him swallow hard—of nine months.

The last year had been more of an adventure than anything he had encountered with the agency.

"Just a couple more," Mimi promised.

But Belle apparently had decided she'd endured more than enough. "My doggies!" she said, her chin jutting out with plenty of East's stubbornness.

She squirmed and fought, the ruffled yellow dress Easton had dressed her in for the occasion proving too slick for him to keep hold of her very well.

"Let me try," Easton said.

He willingly surrendered his squirmy armful. Easton took their daughter, her sleek blond hair brushing Belle's dark curls as she leaned in close to whisper something in her ear.

What she said must have tickled Belle. She giggled,

just about the sweetest sound he knew, but obediently froze in her mother's arm until Mimi could snap off a few more shots.

"These are perfect. Okay, now give Belle to Tess. I want to take a few of you and East alone," Mimi ordered.

"You don't need to do that," Easton protested.

"I want to. When you have nothing but gray hairs from keeping track of your teenager, you might want to look back on the day you officially became parents."

They officially became parents six years ago. He thought of that memorial up in the mountains and the tiny grave in Denver he and Easton and Belle had visited together at Christmastime.

And they were going to give Belle a younger brother or sister again in roughly seven months, though nobody else knew that yet.

He watched Easton carry Belle over to where Tess played with her and Quinn's son, Joe, and Mimi and Brant's daughter, Abigail. The three toddlers shrieked and giggled and headed immediately toward poor Suzy and her puppies.

His heart swelled, watching them all. He and East had talked about waiting another year or so before adding to their family, but her unexpected pregnancy still had thrilled both of them. They had decided not to tell anyone else for now and he loved this secret between them, the shared glances, the furtive smiles, this low hum of anticipation that seemed to follow him everywhere.

He would be here through every stage of this pregnancy, unlike her last one, and he intended to savor every second.

"Nice turnout, isn't it?" Mimi said

He followed her gaze to the crowd filling the Winder Ranch back garden, at all their friends and neighbors who had turned out for the party.

"It's wonderful," he said. This impromptu fiesta hadn't exactly been planned either. But Quinn and Brant had surprised them and brought their families in from Seattle and Los Angeles as a show of solidarity during the final adoption proceedings. Mimi and Tess between them had worked out the details of throwing a big barbecue.

He was amazed at all the people from Pine Gluch who had come out to celebrate with them. All the Dalton brothers were there and Jenna and Carson McRaven and their family. Even Nate and Emery Cavazos had brought their daughters, though Emery, the Daltons' adored half-sister, was hugely pregnant and looked ready to go into labor any minute.

East had also insisted they invite Belle's aunt, Sharon, and her husband and children and John's mother, Judy, with whom they had stayed in frequent contact this past year. He had wondered if John's family would feel uncomfortable around these people they didn't know, but they were currently deep in conversation with Caroline Dalton, who could put anyone at ease.

Children shrieked and laughed as they played boccie ball on a stretch of lawn, a couple of old-timers were arguing local politics at one table and the women setting out the buffet table were laughing hard at something Maggie Dalton's mother, Viviana, said.

It was crazy and chaotic and noisy and he couldn't imagine anywhere he would rather be.

Brant and Quinn were busy at the big half-barrel

barbecue, grilling up some of the Winder Ranch prime grade A steaks. Any minute now, he expected them to start nagging him to get over there and help them out.

Despite his assurances to Easton when he asked her to marry him, he hadn't quite known what reaction to expect from his foster brothers. Brant had stared at him for a long moment and then gave that slow, solemn smile of his before reaching out to shake his hand. Quinn, on the other hand, had been the one to smack him on the back of the head and ask what the hell had taken him so long.

He had worried things might be awkward between the four of them with the new dynamic of him and Easton being together, but they had all slipped into the changing relationship as easily as one of Guff's hand-tied gray nymphs at the end of a fly rod dancing into the waters of Windy Lake.

Easton returned from settling Belle and he wrapped his arms around her and pulled her against him, inhaling the springtime scent of wildflowers that always clung to her hair and her skin.

"Perfect." Mimi smiled, her camera clicking rapidly. "You two are perfect just like that."

They were, he thought, as they posed for a few more photographs. The last year had been full of more joy than he ever thought possible.

"Did you get enough?" Easton asked a few moments later. "I should probably go make sure everything's running smoothly in the kitchen."

"For now," Mimi said. "When things settle down a little, I want to get some shots of just you and Belle and then maybe Cisco and Belle. I'll find you later. I want to get some candids of Belle with her cousins and those adorable dogs before Suzy loses her patience."

"Thanks, Mimi." Easton smiled at her, then sighed with relief when the other woman walked away.

"I hate cameras," she muttered. "You'd think Mimi would have a little compassion, after all those years of having the paparazzi chasing after her."

"A little sacrifice will be worth it," he answered. "Won't it be nice to be able to remember today?"

Her blue eyes softened. "You're right. You're so right. It's been a great day, hasn't it?"

"The best ever."

She wrapped her arms around him for a quick embrace and he rested his chin on her head for just a moment, at peace here with her in his arms as he was nowhere else. "The best day so far in a year of best days," she answered softly. "And something tells me we've got plenty more in store for us."

She was right. He could look ahead to more parties like this one, to more moonlight rides up into the mountains, to roundup and spring planting and the magic of the first winter snow.

"Today I'm content with this one," he murmured and kissed her. As always, her mouth offered sweet, warm welcome.

After a moment, she pulled away reluctantly. "As much as I'd love to stand here all evening and do this, I really have to go see what's happening in the kitchen."

"Yeah, and I'd better help Quinn and Brant with grill duty or I'll never hear the end of it."

He watched her walk through the crowd gathered at Winder Ranch, her smile bright as she paused now and again to greet people, to kiss old Guillermo Cruz on the cheek, to laugh at something Carson McRaven said to her.

As he watched her with their neighbors and friends, he touched a finger to the *E* at the edge of the tattoo on his forearm, something he realized he rarely did anymore.

He supposed he didn't need a compass rose to show him the way home anymore.

He was already there.

* * * * *

 Silhouette®

COMING NEXT MONTH

Available October 26, 2010

SPECIAL EDITION®

REQUEST YOUR FREE BOOKS!

2 FREE NOVELS PLUS 2 FREE GIFTS!

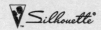

SPECIAL EDITION

Life, Love and Family!

YES! Please send me 2 FREE Silhouette® Special Edition® novels and my 2 FREE gifts (gifts are worth about $10). After receiving them, if I don't wish to receive any more books, I can return the shipping statement marked "cancel." If I don't cancel, I will receive 6 brand-new novels every month and be billed just $4.24 per book in the U.S. or $4.99 per book in Canada. That's a saving of 15% off the cover price! It's quite a bargain! Shipping and handling is just 50¢ per book.* I understand that accepting the 2 free books and gifts places me under no obligation to buy anything. I can always return a shipment and cancel at any time. Even if I never buy another book from Silhouette, the two free books and gifts are mine to keep forever.

235/335 SDN E5RG

Name _____ (PLEASE PRINT) _____

Address _____ Apt. # _____

City _____ State/Prov. _____ Zip/Postal Code _____

Signature (if under 18, a parent or guardian must sign)

Mail to the Silhouette Reader Service:
IN U.S.A.: P.O. Box 1867, Buffalo, NY 14240-1867
IN CANADA: P.O. Box 609, Fort Erie, Ontario L2A 5X3

Not valid for current subscribers to Silhouette Special Edition books.

Want to try two free books from another line?
Call 1-800-873-8635 or visit www.morefreebooks.com.

* Terms and prices subject to change without notice. Prices do not include applicable taxes. N.Y. residents add applicable sales tax. Canadian residents will be charged applicable provincial taxes and GST. Offer not valid in Quebec. This offer is limited to one order per household. All orders subject to approval. Credit or debit balances in a customer's account(s) may be offset by any other outstanding balance owed by or to the customer. Please allow 4 to 6 weeks for delivery. Offer available while quantities last.

Your Privacy: Silhouette is committed to protecting your privacy. Our Privacy Policy is available online at www.eHarlequin.com or upon request from the Reader Service. From time to time we make our lists of customers available to reputable third parties who have a product or service of interest to you. If you would prefer we not share your name and address, please check here. ☐

Help us get it right—We strive for accurate, respectful and relevant communications. To clarify or modify your communication preferences, visit us at www.ReaderService.com/consumerschoice.

SSE10R

HARLEQUIN®

A *Romance*

FOR EVERY MOOD™

Spotlight on

Inspirational

Wholesome romances
that touch the heart and soul.

See the next page
to enjoy a sneak peek from
the Love Inspired® Suspense
inspirational series.

*See below for a sneak peek from
our inspirational line, Love Inspired® Suspense*

*Enjoy this heart-stopping excerpt from
RUNNING BLIND
by top author Shirlee McCoy,
available November 2010!*

**The mission trip to Mexico was supposed to be an
adventure. But the thrill turns sour when Jenna Dougherty
and her roommate Magdalena are kidnapped.**

"It's okay. I'm here to help." The voice was as deep as the
darkness, but Jenna Dougherty didn't believe the lie. She
could do nothing but lie still as hands slid down her arms,
felt the rope around her wrists.

"I'm going to use a knife to cut you free, Jenna. Hold
still."

The cold blade of a knife pressed close to her head before
her gag fell away.

"I—" she started, but her mouth was dry, and she could
do nothing but suck in air.

"Shhh. Whatever needs to be said can be said when
we're out of here." Nick spoke quietly, his hand gentle on
her cheek. There and gone as he sliced through the ropes on
her wrists and ankles.

He pulled her upright. "Come on. We may be on
borrowed time."

"I can't leave my friend," Jenna rasped out.

"There's no one here. Just us."

"She has to be here." Jenna took a step away.

"There's no one here. Let's go before that changes."

"It's dark. Maybe if we find a light…"

"What did you say?"

"We need to turn on the light. I can't leave until I know that—"

"What can you see, Jenna?"

"Nothing."

"No shadows? No light?"

"No."

"It's broad daylight. There's light spilling in from the window I climbed in through. You can't see it?"

She went cold at his words.

"I can't see anything."

"You've got a nasty bruise on your forehead. Maybe that has something to do with it." His fingers traced the tender flesh on her forehead.

"It doesn't matter *how* it happened. I'm blind!"

Can Nick help Jenna find her friend or will chasing this trail have Jenna running blindly again into danger?

Find out in RUNNING BLIND, available in November 2010 only from Love Inspired Suspense.

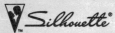

ROMANTIC
SUPENSE
Sparked by Danger, Fueled by Passion.

DEADLIER
— *than the* —
MALE

BY *NEW YORK TIMES* AND
USA TODAY BESTSELLING AUTHOR

SHARON
SALA

AND
COLLEEN THOMPSON

Women can be dangerous enemies
but love will conquer all.

Available November wherever books are sold.

Visit Silhouette Books at www.eHarlequin.com

SRS27701